Advance Praise for *The Indifferen*

"A *Big Chill* for Gen X & Gen Y, this love letter to
the new Lost Generation is funny, sexy, uplifting, and
refreshingly free of pretentiousness and cynicism. *The
Indifference League* is a wild ride and a compelling treat
that reveals the inner superhero in all of us."
— HEATHER J. WOOD,
AUTHOR OF *FORTUNE COOKIE*

"*The Indifference League* is a perfect satiric cocktail: mix
two parts hilarious send-up of pop culture with one part
sharp observations about relationships, add a splash of sex
and a twist of compassion. Don't miss this book."
— SUSAN JUBY,
AUTHOR OF *THE WOEFIELD POULTRY COLLECTIVE*

"*The Big Chill* meets Marvel Comics in Richard Scarsbrook's
smart, funny take on Gen Y's transition to adulthood. Who
did we want to be and who did we become? are the hard
questions at the heart of this coming-of-middle-age tale."
— ALLAN STRATTON,
AUTHOR OF *THE RESURRECTION OF MARY MABEL MCTAVISH*

"*The Indifference League* sizzles with energy
and humour as it romps through the reunion
weekend of quirky high school friends."
— PATRICIA WESTERHOF,
AUTHOR OF *THE DOVE IN BATHURST STATION*

THE INDIFFERENCE LEAGUE

RICHARD SCARSBROOK

DUNDURN
TORONTO

Editor: Shannon Whibbs
Design: Courtney Horner
Printer: Webcom
Cover design by Jesse Hooper
Cover image: © MenagerieCreative
Author photo: Danielle McMann

Library and Archives Canada Cataloguing in Publication

Scarsbrook, Richard, author
          The indifference league / Richard Scarsbrook.

Issued in print and electronic formats.
ISBN 978-1-4597-1036-8

          I. Title.

PS8587.C396I53 2014   C813'.54   C2013-908359-6
                                               C2013-908360-X

1   2   3   4   5   18   17   16   15   14

We acknowledge the support of the **Canada Council for the Arts** and the **Ontario Arts Council** for our publishing program. We also acknowledge the financial support of the **Government of Canada** through the **Canada Book Fund** and **Livres Canada Books**, and the **Government of Ontario** through the **Ontario Book Publishing Tax Credit** and the **Ontario Media Development Corporation**.

Care has been taken to trace the ownership of copyright material used in this book. The author and the publisher welcome any information enabling them to rectify any references or credits in subsequent editions.
                                                                              J. Kirk Howard, President

The publisher is not responsible for websites or their content unless they are owned by the publisher.

Visit us at
Dundurn.com
@dundurnpress
Facebook.com/dundurnpress
Pinterest.com/dundurnpress

Dundurn
3 Church Street, Suite 500
Toronto, Ontario, Canada
M5E 1M2

Gazelle Book Services Limited
White Cross Mills
High Town, Lancaster, England
LA1 4XS

Dundurn
2250 Military Road
Tonawanda, NY
U.S.A. 14150

This book is for
Bluebell
and
for all of my real-life
Super Friends

*"To fight Injustice. To right that which is wrong.
And to serve all mankind!"*

— SLOGAN FROM THE TV SERIES
SUPER FRIENDS, 1973–1974

CONTENTS

THE ORIGINAL EIGHT!!!
AND THEIR ROLE MODELS!

THE STATISTICIAN
Albert Einstein
(Theoretical Physicist)

HIPPIE AVENGER
Georgia O'Keeffe
(Artist, embraced by 1960s
feminists for her "vaginal"
paintings of flowers)

THE DRIFTER
Aquaman
(Fictional Superhero)

PSYCHO SUPERSTAR
Ted Nugent
(Rock Guitarist, "The
Motor City Madman")

SUPERKEN
George S. Patton
(U.S. General,
"Man of Destiny")

MISS DEMEANOR
Joan Jett
(Punk Rock Singer, Leader
of The Blackhearts)

SUPERBARBIE
Mary
(Mother of Jesus Christ)

MR. NICE GUY
Marty McFly
(Fictional Character from
the movie *Back to the Future*)

Collector Card #1 — *Collect All 20!*

1/20

MR. NICE GUY

"Here I come to save the day!"

— Mighty Mouse, from the TV series
Mighty Mouse Playhouse, 1955–1966

SUPERHERO PROFILE: MR. NICE GUY

A.K.A.: Buddy, Dude, Pal

SEX: Male **HEIGHT:** 5'5" **WEIGHT:** 140 pounds

CIVILIAN ROLE: Archivist, Toronto Public Library

SPECIAL POWERS:
Extreme Empathy.

SPECIAL EQUIPMENT:
Super G Digital Athletic Chronometer
with Built-in Calculator!

SPECIAL VEHICLE:
Grey Honda Civic (Base Model).

FAVOURED ELIXIR:
"Whatever everyone else is having!"

SLOGAN/MANTRA:
"Whatever everyone else wants!"

THE INDIFFERENCE LEAGUE

DID YOU KNOW?
Mr. Nice Guy has a scar on his left testicle from being kicked by SuperKen (who was wearing cleats) during a gym-class soccer game in grade nine. The injury was ruled an accident by the gym teacher, despite the fact that Mr. Nice Guy was not in possession of the ball at the time.

Collector Card #2 — *Collect All 20!*

2/20

Mr. Nice Guy is typing an email invitation to the other members of The Indifference League:

> **To: *statistician; hippieavenger; missde-meanor69; thedrifter; theperfectpair***
>
> **Subject: The Brat Signal™ is ON!!!!!!!!**
>
> Greetings, Lads and Lasses,
> Given that our collective thirtieth birthdays are rapidly approaching, I am activating the Brat Signal™!!!!!
>
> To commemorate this milestone year, all surviving members of The Indifference League ™ are hereby summoned to The Hall of Indifference™ for the upcoming holiday long weekend!

As so often happens these days, his mind drifts back nearly twelve years, to the night that they collectively became known as The Indifference League.

*

It is a warm, starry evening on the Sunday of the July long weekend, and Mr. Nice Guy and his friends are hanging out on the stony beach in front of his parents' cottage.

(He is not yet known as Mr. Nice Guy; none of them have their alter-ego names yet. It will happen later this night.)

They are gathered around a campfire that has been fuelled to ridiculous roaring heights by Psycho Superstar, with gasoline siphoned from the lawn mower, kerosene drained from the antique lamps inside the cottage, and flammable flotsam and jetsam scavenged from the beach.

On the end of a straightened wire coat hanger, The Statistician is holding a bratwurst sausage in the flames. He swings the crackling, blackened meatsicle over in front of Hippie Avenger and says, "Want it? I swear it's a veggie sausage."

She wrinkles her nose. "Like, yuck."

"Um, I'll take it," Mr. Nice Guy intervenes, sliding the bobbing sausage from the wire with an enriched-white Wonderbread hotdog bun. The bratwurst crunches as he bites into it, and he says, "Mmmmmmm … gasoliney-delicious!"

"*Thankyouverrymuch*," says Psycho Superstar, in a voice approximating the already-dead Elvis Presley's. He tosses a cupful of kerosene into the fire.

(None of them are actually known by their alter-ego nicknames at this point, but this is Mr. Nice Guy's memory, and his mind can retroactively modify anything that it wants to. It's possible that it wasn't even Mr. Nice Guy who saved Hippie Avenger from that hot dog, but he remembers that it was.)

Hippie Avenger gazes up at the tiny lights blinking in the sky, and dreamily muses, "The pilots of those airplanes can, like, probably see this fire from up there."

Psycho Superstar takes this as a compliment, and heaves a broken Styrofoam cooler onto the blaze, proclaiming, "I want this fire to be fuckin' seen from *space*!"

SuperBarbie, from her perch on SuperKen's lap atop an army-surplus Field Marshal's chair, says, "That is *not* good for the environment."

"Tell that to all the industries your dad owns stock in, huh?" Psycho Superstar counters, as the Styrofoam begins to distort and melt. "Though you might have to settle for wearing cheaper shoes, then."

SuperKen's deep voice resonates like a cannon blast. "The quality of the air we breathe is *everyone's* responsibility."

As the captain of the Varsity football, soccer, and hockey teams at Tom Thomson High, the president of the Student Council, the lead tenor in the school choir, and the co-chairperson of T.N.T. (the clever acronym for Teens Need Truth, the Christian prayer club at school), SuperKen is the uncontested alpha male of the group. Usually, none of the other guys would ever contradict him, at least not to his face, but Psycho Superstar won't let it go this time.

"Remember your *responsibility to the environment* when you're dropping fucking *bombs* on it, dude. One bomb is worse than a *hundred* bonfires."

SuperKen is attending the Royal Military College in the fall. He has already been fitted for his dress uniform.

"He is correct," The Statistician says, after a moment of hesitation. He is normally reluctant to embrace any position taken by Psycho Superstar, but The Statistician has harboured a grudge against SuperKen since the graduating class awards were announced a few weeks earlier. Sure, SuperKen deserved to win Male Athlete of the Year, and probably even the school spirit award, but The Statistician suspects that one of the coaches or some starstruck female teacher must have exaggerated a grade or two for SuperKen to have beaten him for the highest academic achievement award.

"The airborne gaseous and particulate contaminants released by the detonation of a single conventional firebomb," The Statistician explains, "would indeed outweigh those created by a burning Styrofoam cooler, by a ratio of about ten thousand to one."

The Statistician has no idea if his estimate is even close to correct, but who is going to argue with him? He was careful to use that lovely mathematician's qualifier, *about*.

"Yeah," adds Psycho Superstar, invigorated by The Statistician's unexpected support, "and burning forests and buildings … and *bodies* … that ain't so good for the air quality, either, Sergeant Rock."

SuperBarbie glares at Psycho Superstar and The Statistician.

"Not every man can wear the uniform, y'know," she snaps. "Not every man has what it takes."

SuperBarbie has been SuperKen's girlfriend since grade nine. They've exchanged promise rings, and SuperBarbie has a hope chest in her bedroom, which she fills with the kitschy dust-collectors that SuperKen gives her as gifts.

Despite having a figure as similar as biology will allow to her anatomically impossible fashion-doll namesake, when SuperBarbie ties her hair back in a ponytail and squashes her breasts into a body-armour-grade sports bra, she is a tremendous athlete. In addition to being the captain of the women's varsity volleyball and softball teams, SuperBarbie also set new city records in the 100- and 200-metre dashes. She stood right next to SuperKen at the graduating class awards ceremony with her Female Athlete of the Year trophy in hand. She is also the treasurer and secretary of the student council, the lead soprano in the school choir, and the co-chairperson of Teens Need Truth.

SuperBarbie is SuperKen's female mirror image in every way, his ultimate counterpart. Although some of their inferiors have sarcastically referred to them as "The Perfect Pair," they nevertheless earned enough votes to be named king and queen of the senior prom at Tom Thomson High.

"Not every man has the courage to stand up and fight for their God and their country," SuperBarbie reiterates, flipping her ponytail at Psycho Superstar and The Statistician.

"Well, god*damn* it, Hot Lips," says Miss Demeanor, drawing from her encyclopedic memory for pop-culture quotes, "resign your *goddamned* commission!"

"*M*A*S*H*, right?" The Drifter says. "Good one!"

"My *commission*!" Miss Demeanor bawls. "My *commission*!"

"Idiots!" SuperBarbie hisses through clenched teeth.

"It's okay, baby," says SuperKen, patting her behind. "Let them have their fun."

SuperBarbie emphatically kisses SuperKen, and for a moment they resemble the picture of Ingrid Bergman and Humphrey Bogart on that famous movie poster for *Casablanca*, or maybe Vivien Leigh and Clark Gable in *Gone with the Wind*. You can almost hear the orchestral soundtrack billowing up around them.

"Thanks!" Psycho Superstar says. "Permission for fun!"

He tosses more kerosene and beach garbage onto the fire and the column of flame roars skyward like the afterburner trail of a fighter jet.

"Your nickname should be 'Smokey,' baby," Miss Demeanor suggests.

"Well, there's already Smokey Robinson, Smokey Bear, Smokey and the Bandit," the Statistician says. "Not too original, perhaps."

They are all very concerned with being "original." Hence The Statistician's professorial Harris Tweed jacket, the way he says "indeed" and "perhaps" all the time. Hence Hippie Avenger's sandals, her flower-printed smocks, and her, like, Flower Child way of talking. Hence Psycho Superstar's testicle-gripping, intentionally-ripped black jeans, his collection of heavy-metal concert T-shirts festooned with skulls and demons, and the way he uses obscenities like punctuation. Hence Miss Demeanor's blood-red lipstick, her needle-straight she-vampire hair, and the faux-leather miniskirt that barely covers her crotch, in which she sits with her legs slightly parted, daring you to look.

SuperKen and SuperBarbie feel no need to differentiate their appearances from others; their *accomplishments* set them apart from the crowd. The Perfect Pair dress them-selves in the sort of clothing seen on any of the statistically perfect models from the current year's Sears catalogue. At the moment, they are wearing matching "cottage clothes," with little ducks — or maybe they're loons — embroidered on their crew-neck sweaters and khaki pants.

"Too bad," says Psycho Superstar. The handful of dry leaves he's thrown crackle and vanish in the orange roar. "I like the sound of 'Smokey'!"

"What about 'Pyro,' then?" Miss Demeanor says. "Nobody's taken that one yet."

"Some comic book superhero's named Pyro," The Drifter says. "One of the X-Men, I think."

Of course, The Drifter doesn't *think* Pyro is one of the X-Men; he *knows*. But, as the youngest of the bunch, two years junior to the rest of the gang, he's not so sure that his encyclopedic knowledge of comic-book characters and plotlines is considered very cool anymore, especially since his older brother, The Statistician, just won all those university entrance scholarships.

"The X-Men *suck*," says Psycho Superstar, as he searches around with a flashlight for more flammable items to throw on his Monument to Combustion. "Give me the good ol' Super Friends any day of the week. Superman, Batman and Robin, Wonder Woman …"

"Don't forget Zan and Jayna, the Wonder Twins!" Miss Demeanor interrupts.

She and Psycho Superstar punch knuckles, mimicking the ring-touching gesture that initiated the superpowers of the Wonder Twins; it's no secret that the two of them have been having a *thing* together.

"*Wonder Twin Powers, Activate!*" Miss Demeanor squeals. "Form of …"

"A Steely Dan Brand stainless-steel dildo!" Psycho Superstar hollers. "Form of …"

"A tube of KY personal lubricant!" Miss Demeanor responds.

It is also no secret that Psycho Superstar and Miss Demeanor have been having quite an *adventurous* thing.

"Zan and Jayna *sucked*," The Statistician grumbles. "The chick always got to transform into something cool, like a jaguar or a falcon, while the guy always turned into something useless, like a bucket of water or a rain cloud."

Of course The Statistician is trying to be inflammatory; he would normally never use a word like "chick"; as the former captain of the Tom Thomson High School intramural debating team, The Statistician is always up for an argument, even when he knows he's on the lower ground.

"Feminist bullshit," SuperKen says.

"Hey!" yelps Miss Demeanor.

"Yeah, seriously," Mr. Nice Guy adds.

"Look, guys," Hippie Avenger says. "Feminism isn't a bad word, okay? It came along at a time when, like, women didn't have the *vote*, when we were considered, like, *property*, for Chrissakes."

"Yeah," Mr. Nice Guy reiterates.

"Feminists are just man-haters," SuperBarbie says, rolling her eyes, and then tightening her arms around SuperKen's neck.

"I'm a feminist," Hippie Avenger protests, "but I'm definitely not a 'man-hater.'"

"Or women who can't *get* a man," SuperBarbie adds.

"Hey," Mr. Nice Guy says. "She's got me!"

"Exactly," SuperKen says, flexing the muscles in his arms as he gropes SuperBarbie. "She couldn't attract a *man*."

"Troglodyte!" Mr. Nice Guy wants to say (but doesn't).

"*I'm* a feminist," Miss Demeanor says, raising an eyebrow at SuperBarbie. "Wanna insult *me*, chickie?"

"And she's into *me*," Psycho Superstar adds.

"Well, I'm into your body," Miss Demeanor says, pinching his ass.

20 · RICHARD SCARSBROOK

"I'm okay with that," he says. Then he turns and glares at SuperKen. "So, my lady here is a feminist, Seargent Rock … wanna tell me that *I'm* not a man?"

SuperKen and SuperBarbie glance at each other, and seem to telepathically agree to ignore them; the Male and Female Athletes of the Year may be fitter, but Miss Demeanor and Psycho Superstar have the potential to be a lot meaner in a fight.

"Come on, guys, let's not get personal," The Drifter says.

(Mr. Nice Guy was *going* to say something like this, but The Drifter beat him to it.)

The Drifter figures that his comic-book knowledge will not make him look like a geek in this particular instance, so he says, "This discussion is about Zan and Jayna on *Super Friends*, remember? Zan always turned into things made of water, and Jayna always turned into an *animal*. It's just the way their superpowers worked. There was nothing *political* about it."

"Everything is political," Miss Demeanor says.

"Whatever," SuperKen says, "Jan and Zayna still *sucked*."

"And, no offense, ladies, but as much as I hate to agree with Sergeant Rock," Psycho Superstar adds, "the rest of those add-on, politically correct Super Friends were *bullshit*, too. I mean, *Apache Chief? Samurai? Rima* the fucking *Jungle Girl?* Gimme a break."

Hippie Avenger sighs. "But, like, the creators were just trying to instill some cultural sensitivity into their young viewers, at a time when, like …"

"Then they should have created culturally sensitive characters that didn't *suck ass!*" Psycho Superstar says. "The *real* superheroes are the five originals: Superman, Batman and Robin, Wonder Woman, and Aquaman."

"Aquaman is *useless*," The Statistician says, with unexpected emotion. He adapts a Saturday-morning-cartoon-superhero voice. "Superman and Wonder Woman, you two go fly around the world at supersonic speed to prevent the disaster that's been set in motion by the Legion of Doom! Batman and Robin, you guys get your asses into the Batmobile and stop the villains from escaping their lair! And Aquaman … uhhhhhh, yeah … *Aquaman.* Um, what are your superpowers again? Oh. Right. Um, then you go for a *swim,* okay? And while you're in there, you should have a *talk* with your friends *the fishies.* Yes, you go do *that.* That'll really help."

Everyone laughs, except for The Drifter. He takes a slurp from his beer and mutters, "I *like* Aquaman."

The Drifter is the closest thing to a real-live Aquaman in the group. He was on the Tom Thomson High School junior swim team in grade nine, but he wasn't allowed back in grade ten because of his lacklustre grades. From the beach here at Mr. Nice Guy's parents' cottage, The Drifter can swim all the way out to the island and back.

"Aquaman," The Statistician pronounces, "is *useless.*"

"Fuckin' right," Psycho Superstar agrees. "*Robin* could beat him in a fight. The friggin' *Boy Wonder.* Hell, Batman's *butler* would kick Aquaman's ass."

"Not in the *water,*" The Drifter says, his eyes narrowing. "The neutered, Saturday-morning-cartoon version of Aquaman we all saw on *Super Friends* wasn't a fair representation of the King of Atlantis! I mean, in *Superman vs. Aquaman*, Aquaman took down Superman by flooding his lungs with water, then …"

He stops, and his face flushes red. He's crossed the Dork Line yet again.

The Statistician laughs. "You'd better put away the comic books and start hitting the textbooks, little brother."

"Stop calling me 'little brother.'"

"It's what you are."

"Fuck off. I'm just as big as you are."

"What? Are you gonna go tell the fishies on me?"

Hippie Avenger, who can't swim at all, has already consumed a six-pack of strawberry-flavoured vodka coolers, and she always gets sentimental or amorous (or both) when she's drunk. She throws her arms around The Drifter (who is momentarily distracted from his funk by the feel of her braless breasts against him), and she says, "All of you guys are, like, *my* Super Friends!"

"More like the *Super Dorks*," The Statistician says, rolling his eyes, hoping to deflect yet another maudlin, tearful, it's-our-last-summer-together moment. "Perhaps we should call ourselves the *Not-So-Super Friends*."

"You're such a dick," The Drifter mutters.

Without unlocking his gaze from the second bratwurst sausage he's scorching, The Statistician says, "Perhaps *you* should shut up and go study for your remedial summer-school courses, *little brother*."

The Drifter jumps up, fists clenched.

"Hey now, boys," says SuperKen, in that fighter-pilot voice of his, "calm down, now. I don't want to have to intervene."

The Statistician turns and glares at SuperKen. "What are you, the United Nations Security Council? Perhaps you should mind your own business."

"Yeah," The Drifter says. "This is between us. Go back to fondling the Female Athlete of the Year."

"Hey," SuperKen says, easing his grip on one of Super-Barbie's breasts. "Watch it."

Mr. Nice Guy feels obligated to ease the tension by saying something funny, so in his best Ted Knight voice (who did the narration for the *Super Friends* cartoon on Saturday morning TV), he cries out the motto: "*To fight Injustice. To right that which is wrong. And to serve all mankind!*"

Again The Statistician rolls his eyes. "Perhaps our motto should be: To *talk about* how *somebody else* should do something about Injustice! To *get drunk* while *discussing* right and wrong! And to eat *bratwurst* while doing it!"

He thrusts the scorched sausage in the air, brandishing the crooked coat-hanger wire like a general leading a cavalry.

"You're *such* a superior being," The Drifter snipes. "The rest of us have *so* much to learn from you."

"Actually," Miss Demeanor says, "he's right. Our *modus operandi* is sitting around together, drinking and eating and throwing bullshit around. We never actually *do* anything"

"And there are probably, like, a thousand other little groups like us all over the Western world," Hippie Avenger ponders. "We've never had a Vietnam to bring us together. Or a Kent State. Or a Woodstock."

"Or a World War One," SuperKen adds. "Or a World War Two."

"Nor a depression, *nor* an inquisition," says The Statistician, in that professorial tone of voice, *"nor* a Renaissance, *nor* a revolution."

"And fucking amen to that!" Psycho Superstar says. "Who needs any of that shit?"

"And fucking amen to that!" Miss Demeanor seconds, grandly raising her bottle in the air. "To *Indifference*!"

"To the Not-So-Super Friends!" Mr. Nice Guy cries, also raising his bottle.

Not wanting to look like the sucky-baby his brother often accuses him of being, The Drifter reluctantly lifts his bottle, too. "To the Indifference League," he says.

"Good one!" says Hippie Avenger.

"Nice," says Miss Demeanor

Mr. Nice Guy shrugs, and mutters, "What about the Not-So-Super Friends?"

"It's good, too, buddy," Hippie Avenger says in that soothing, dovelike voice.

"To the Indifference League!" The Drifter cheers again.

Hippie Avenger, Psycho Superstar, Miss Demeanor, and The Statistician hoist their drinks and repeat the toast in unison. As the co-chairs of Teens Need Truth, the Perfect Pair are still clucking to each other over the blasphemous use of the term "fucking amen," but in the spirit of the moment they join the toast anyway, waving their antifreeze-coloured athletic beverages at the airplanes and stars twinkling overhead.

Bold declarations are made.

"Collectively, from this point forward," Hippie Avenger says, "we will be known formally as *The Indifference League*, and informally as the *Not-So-Super Friends*. All those in agreement, say 'Aye'!"

"Aye!" the others cry.

"My cottage," Mr. Nice Guy declares, "will be henceforth known as *The Hall of Indifference*. We will all pledge to meet here at least once a year for the rest of our lives. All those in agreement, say 'Yeah'!"

They all cry "Yeah," even The Statistician, who is pretty sure that he will soon be moving on to Bigger and Better Things.

"Signed, the Breakfast Club," says Miss Demeanor.

"Another good one," the Drifter affirms. "You rock, Molly Ringwald."

"I'm more like the fucked-up Ally Sheedy character, I think," says Miss Demeanor, as she reaches stroke the crotch of Psycho Superstar's shredded jeans. "But I *do* rock."

"Oh, baby, you *k*nowwwwww what ah like!" Psycho Superstar croons, Big Bopper style, placing his hands behind his head and performing several spastic pelvic thrusts.

The Perfect Pair look away in disgust, even though SuperBarbie has been casually grinding SuperKen's erection between her gym-toned butt cheeks all evening.

Her wine-cooler-fuelled euphoria unrestrained, Hippie Avenger cheers, "Now, like, all we need are superhero names!"

Since they are aware that everyone calls them Ken and Barbie behind their backs, anyway, The Perfect Pair are good sports about it. They simply add the prefix "Super" to their nicknames, and then they run off giggling into the cottage, where they will kiss and fondle and suck and stroke and finger each other, but they will not have actual intercourse, since they have promised God (via the Teens Need Truth club) that they will wait until their wedding night to consummate their bond.

Mr. Nice Guy and Hippie Avenger invent one another's Indifference League names. They have been dating for the past couple of months, and they're going to the senior prom together; they have not yet stumbled upon Just the Right Moment to have sex with each other, though.

As far as the rest of the gang can tell, Miss Demeanor is not so much *dating* Psycho Superstar as simply exchanging bodily fluids with him. Nevertheless, she is so moved when Psycho Superstar names her after his second-favourite rock song (a track from the *Kim Mitchell* EP), that she jumps up and hugs him, kissing him on both cheeks. Miss Demeanor's lips have spent much time on other parts of Psycho Superstar's body, but she's never kissed him *there* before. Her lips normally hit him like punches, like challenges, but these ones are more like whispers. He has to holler *"Fuckin' RIGHT!"* at the top of his lungs just to keep things in balance.

Without girlfriends or sex buddies to assist them in selecting their own alter-ego titles, The Statistician and The Drifter pick their own. The other Not-So-Super Friends agree that their new aliases suit them.

The Indifference League spends the rest of the night becoming superheroically intoxicated.

"Hey, Statistician!" The Drifter calls out, now full of cheap, sweet beer and renewed brotherly love, "Cook me up another bratwurst, wouldja?"

"Indeed," The Statistician replies, "but first you've got to activate the Brat Signal."

It's a pretty good joke for The Statistician.

Mr. Nice Guy smiles drunkenly at the stars; even if the other members of The Indifference League don't realize it yet, he knows that the day that has just passed by will be a defining moment for all of them, that they have just formed the sort of esoteric bond that keeps friends together for the rest of their lives.

And it happened *here*, at *his* cottage, because of *him*.

I am happy, he tells himself. *All is well. Yeah.*

Mr. Nice Guy glances at his watch, his most prized possession: *The Super G Digital Athletic Chronometer*. It has a built-in calculator and everything; it's as if he's got the instrument cluster from a fighter jet strapped to his wrist.

The Super G reads 12:11 a.m. Eleven minutes past midnight. It's tomorrow already.

The day that has just passed also happened to be his eighteenth birthday. None of them remembered, not even Hippie Avenger.

It doesn't matter, he tells himself. *It's okay. It was a good day anyway.*

When Psycho Superstar turned eighteen last month, they all chipped in for a bottle of rye whiskey for him, and he got to grope both Miss Demeanor's and Hippie Avenger's bodies when they complied with his request for "a birthday babe sandwich."

For Mr. Nice Guy's birthday, nobody even passed a card around for everyone to sign.

But it's okay. Mr. Nice Guy doesn't mind.

He is happy. All is well.

*

There is a pensive smile on Mr. Nice Guy's face as he floats up from this old memory and resurfaces in the present, where his fingers are still hovering over the keyboard of his outdated computer.

It never happened again. Despite Mr. Nice Guy's consistent efforts, that weekend twelve years ago was the last time that they were all together in the same place at the same time — well, except for the funeral, of course. Sure, a few of the other Not-So-Super Friends would show up at The Hall of Indifference from year to year, but never everyone, and sometimes no one at all.

This year will be different, Mr. Nice Guy thinks. He can feel it. This year, everyonce will come. He blinks, blinks again, and then continues typing.

> Of course, the invitation is also extended to everyone's significant others.

The Statistician's moody, passive-aggressive wife was inducted into The Indifference League a few years ago, but Mr. Nice Guy doesn't dare mention in the email the *nom de plume* that he and Hippie Avenger invented for her: Time Bomb.

Miss Demeanor and The Drifter have taken to calling her that, too, but never in front of The Statistician, and especially not to Time Bomb herself, who could go off at any moment, without warning.

Mr. Nice Guy stabs at the keyboard again.

> The Drifter, Hippie Avenger and Miss Demeanor, invite your current main squeezes along if you've got 'em, and we'll initiate them into the League.

Mr. Nice Guy leans against the backrest of his faux-leather desk chair, hoping that either Miss Demeanor or Hippie Avenger shows up solo; lately he has found himself wondering if, under the right circumstances, some of the old magic might return with one of his former girlfriends. It's been a lonely year.

He shakes his head, and types some more.

> Mr. Nice Guy will provide all the booze and

food (especially the bratwurst!). I've bought
new sheets and pillows for The Hall of Indiffer-
ence™, so no need for sleeping bags anymore!

Long Live the Not-So-Super Friends™!!!!!!!
Your Fearless Leader,
Mr. Nice Guy

Of course he will provide everything, the food, the booze,
the lodging. He will pay for it all, without expecting anything in return, even though most of the other Not-So-Super
Friends have higher incomes than he does. Of course he will!
He is Mr. Nice Guy!

Mr. Nice Guy deletes "Your Fearless Leader." SuperKen
will surely make fun of him if he includes that line. He is
about to hit the "Send" button when he notices something
else, in the second paragraph of the email:

To commemorate this milestone year, all surviving members of the Indifference League™ are
hereby summoned to The Hall of Indifference™
for the upcoming holiday long weekend!

He also deletes the word "surviving." No need to reopen
that old wound.

PSYCHO SUPERSTAR

*"Madness, as you know, is like gravity.
All it takes is a little push."*

— THE JOKER, FROM THE MOVIE *THE DARK KNIGHT*, 2008

SUPERHERO PROFILE: PSYCHO SUPERSTAR

A.K.A.: That Prick from the Warehouse

SEX: Male **HEIGHT:** 6'1" **WEIGHT:** 175 pounds

CIVILIAN ROLE: Line Operator, King o' the Bun
condiment factory

SPECIAL POWERS: Rockin', Drinkin', and Kickin' Ass!

SPECIAL EQUIPMENT:
Stainless Steel Switchblade.
Zippo Lighter engraved with skull-and-crossbones.

SPECIAL VEHICLES:
Black Ford F-150 Stepside Pickup Truck (Heavily Modified).
Kawasaki Ninja ZX-14 (Destroyed in Action).

FAVOURED ELIXIR:
Jack Daniels. Or anything else with alcohol in it.

SLOGAN/MANTRA: "Fuckin' right!"

THE INDIFFERENCE LEAGUE

DID YOU KNOW?
Psycho Superstar's silver-chained trucker wallet contained a
strip of three photos of himself and Miss Demeanor, taken
in a photo booth in a suburban shopping mall. In the first
photo they are each giving the camera lens the finger. In
the second, they are French kissing. In the third, they are
blowing smoke rings.

Collector Card #3 — *Collect All 20!*   3/20

Psycho Superstar was the only member of The Indifference League who ever claimed to posses any superpowers: *"Rockin', Drinkin', and Kickin' Ass."*

He got his name from a song by Ron Hawkins — not the old country music star "Rompin'" Ronnie Hawkins, but the Toronto indie scene legend who was the frontman for the Lowest of the Low. Psycho Superstar loved all of those indie rock bands; he'd seen them all at least a dozen times each at The Horseshoe and Lee's Palace and Sneaky Dee's. But he loved Ron Hawkins the best.

During the four years that followed their graduation from Tom Thomson High School, Psycho Superstar was the wealthiest of the Not-So-Super Friends. While The Drifter laboured on for two more years in high school, then left to go backpacking through Europe and Asia, and the other members of The Indifference League lived the starving-student lifestyle in various university residences, Psycho Superstar landed a high-paying job on the jar-capping line at the King o' the Bun condiment factory.

While the rest of them subsisted on peanut-butter sandwiches, Kraft Dinner, and whatever discount-brand beer happened to be on sale that week, Psycho Superstar ate at sit-down restaurants and developed an appreciation for Scotch whiskey. He rented a Babe Lair bachelor apartment near the Entertainment District, and he splurged on a blood-red crotch-rocket motorcycle. He'd almost bought the Suzuki GSX-R1000, because the slogan for the bike was Own the Racetrack, and baby, he was ready to own the racetrack, the highway, and anything else he wanted. But then he saw an ad for the Kawasaki Ninja ZX-14, which proclaimed it *"The Most Powerful Production Motorcycle of All Time."*

Ninja. Zed Ex Fourteen. The words tasted like chocolate-coated hallucinogens in his mouth. Now *that* was the name of a Superhero's ride. He paid cash for the bike, and rode it away from the dealership that same day.

There was no doubt about it: Psycho Superstar was *The Man*. As if there was ever any doubt.

*

Four years later, things changed.

SuperKen graduated from the Royal Military College with a degree in military and strategic studies, and joined the Canadian Armed Forces as an officer cadet. While SuperKen's athletic career dwindled somewhat at RMC, since practically everyone else there was *also* the winner of their respective high school's Athlete of the Year Award, SuperBarbie became captain of the Queen's University volleyball team (she had turned down scholarship offers from other universities so she could be close to SuperKen in Kingston). She was being scouted for the Canadian Olympic team, but she passed on that opportunity to begin decorating the Perfect Little Starter Home she and SuperKen purchased near the base where he was stationed, where they would eventually start their Perfect Little Family.

Mr. Nice Guy graduated from the University of Western Ontario with a degree in English and history, and got a job working as an archivist for the Toronto Public Library. Hippie Avenger earned a B.A. in visual arts and women's studies from the University of Guelph, and became the assistant curator of a small but prosperous gallery that sold the works of a semi-famous group of painters from the late sixties.

Miss Demeanor finished her psychology degree at the University of Toronto, where she was hired as a student crisis counsellor. At U of T, she occasionally bumped into The Statistician, who earned a B.Sc. in advanced mathematics, graduated with *Summa Cum Laude* distinction, and won a graduate scholarship in statistics, which allowed him to earn a master's degree and then a Ph.D.

During the summer that the rest of The Indifference League assumed their new Spelled-with-Capital-Letters, University-Degree-Required positions, The Drifter returned from his travels through Europe and Asia, brimming over with stories and knowledge, and a new maturity and self-confidence. The Drifter also brought back with him the motorcycle upon which he'd wandered two continents; not an expensive, overpowered racing bike like Psycho Super-star's, but a battered, ancient Norton Commando, which rumbled and sputtered and barfed blue smoke.

At first Psycho Superstar made fun of The Drifter for the constant repairs and adjustments the Norton required, but the mockery ceased when he noticed that the warhorse bike attracted women to The Drifter like ants to spilled honey. Not even live-for-today Miss Demeanor would climb onto the back of Psycho Superstar's Ninja; the danger outweighed the potential thrill.

*

When the filling lines at the condiment factory shuddered to a halt at the end of another Friday afternoon shift, the last relish jar on Psycho Superstar's conveyor belt was empty, except for the pink slip tucked inside. This was the method favored by the King o' the Bun human resources department for communicating to a line worker that his or her employment had been officially terminated.

That little fucker musta ratted on me to the foreman, Psycho Superstar figured. *It's not like I hurt him. I just shook him up a bit, put him in his place a little.*

He smashed the relish jar against the cinderblock wall, unzipped his pants, and pissed the words FUCK OFF on the concrete warehouse floor, and then he strode out of the factory with his head held high, giving the finger to each of the security cameras along the way. *Fuck 'em all.*

Tonight, Psycho Superstar decided, he would put his superpowers to their ultimate test. So he Rocked. And he Drank. And he Rocked and he Drank some more. And then it was time to go Kick Some Ass.

He climbed onto his Ninja ZX-14 and revved it until it screamed like a hellhound. He pushed that blood-red crotch-rocket to Superhero Velocity; of that there is no doubt. The forensic experts figured he was traveling at over 180 kilometres an hour when he hit the pedestal of that concrete overpass.

They had a difficult time separating the bits of Psycho Superstar from the pieces of the shattered bike. For one thing, everything was the same colour.

*

At the funeral, none of the members of The Indifference League referred to him as Psycho Superstar; they called him "Jake," the name chosen for him by his parents when he was born.

The Statistician puzzled at how the words "dead," "died," and "killed" were carefully avoided. Jake's leather-faced, whiskey-scented father repeated over and over again that he'd "never expected the boy to cash in his chips so soon." SuperBarbie referred to Jake's condition as "asleep in Jesus" and "in God's loving arms," while SuperKen saw him as having "passed over." To Hippie Avenger, Jake had "left us," and to Miss Demeanor, he was merely "gone."

The minister gave a sermon explaining that Jake had "winged his flight from this world, launching himself into eternity." While SuperBarbie called out an emphatic "Amen!" after every line, The Statistician strained against the impulse to roll his eyes, knowing that Jake himself would have said that he'd "bit the dust," "kicked the oxygen habit," "bought the pine condo," or "made a nice road pizza."

Miss Demeanor, the closest thing Jake ever had to a girlfriend, gave the eulogy. She got some sniffling laughs when she recounted the time that Jake got tangled in a barbed-wire fence fleeing from a farmer who had caught him trying to ride the cows. People nodded and chuckled and swatted away tears when Miss Demeanor described that time in high school when the Not-So-Super Friends paid to go bungee jumping from an abandoned railroad bridge over this deep gorge near Guelph. Of course Jake went first. The bungee cord snapped, and he crashed into the water. So, he swam to the shore, climbed the cliff wall back up to the bridge, and demanded a second go for free. It was such a Jake thing to do.

The Drifter gave a short, awkward speech about how Jake was out there right now riding his motorcycle, but instead of just this small, silly world, he now had the whole great big beautiful universe to explore, and he could ride just as fast as he damn well wanted to.

Hippie Avenger tried to read a poem she'd written about Jake, but she couldn't finish it for sobbing. Everyone else joined her.

Mr. Nice Guy couldn't think of anything to say that would make anyone feel any better, so he just sat there frowning at his funeral shoes, feeling guilty about wondering if Jake had also had a *thing* with Hippie Avenger.

It was The Statistician who tiptoed into the little room in the funeral home where the PA system was hidden, and put on a CD with the song "Psycho Superstar," by Ron Hawkins and the Rusty Nails.

In the end, the lyrics didn't have much to do with Jake at all. But it was still a damn good song.

MISS DEMEANOR

"I'm Catwoman. Hear me roar."

— CATWOMAN, FROM THE MOVIE *BATMAN RETURNS*, 1992

A.K.A.: Pussy Purr-fection

SEX: Female **HEIGHT:** 5'6" **WEIGHT:** 135 pounds

CIVILIAN ROLES: Student Crisis Counsellor, University of Toronto; Performer, The Cross/Fire Cabaret

SPECIAL POWERS:
Can change her appearance at will with dozens of costumes and wigs.
Her Self-Defense Class training is also occasionally used offensively.

SPECIAL EQUIPMENT:
Blood-red fingernail extensions.

SPECIAL VEHICLE: Baby-blue Subaru Outback.

FAVOURED ELIXIR:
Gin and Tonic. Or anything else with alcohol in it.

SLOGAN/MANTRA: "You GO, Girlfriend!"

THE INDIFFERENCE LEAGUE

DID YOU KNOW?
The small Chinese symbol on Miss Demeanor's right wrist is identical to the only tattoo Psycho Superstar ever had. Neither of them had any idea what the symbol meant; they just thought it looked cool.

4/20

Miss Demeanor is the first to reply to Mr. Nice Guy's email.

To: *mr_niceguy*

Subject: re: The Brat Signal™ is ON!!!!!!!!

Hey, Buddy,

A collective thirtieth-birthday gathering of the tribe this long weekend sounds like fun. I'll be there for sure – but not until very late on Saturday night or early Sunday morning — I've got a running commitment on Saturday nights.

But maybe before we all get together, you and I could meet in person first. There is something I want to talk to you about — just you — and it's probably best that we do it face to face, without any of the others around.

You name the date and I'll pick the place.

Love,

Miss Demeanor

Mr. Nice Guy's heart races.

Just me. Without any of the others around.

Face to face.

Love, Miss Demeanor
Love.

He emails back immediately and tells her that he's available any night between now and the long weekend.

*

At first, Mr. Nice Guy wonders if he has the right place when Miss Demeanor's typically sketchy directions bring him to an alley off the farthest alien reaches of Queen West. He descends the rusted iron stairs to the basement of the windowless building. The poster on the metal door reads:

This Saturday!

The
Cross/Fire Cabaret
presents

THE
GIRLY–GIRL
BURLESQUE EXTRAVAGANZA!

Featuring:
Marilinn Munrow
Dame Edna Leathertongue
and
Pussy Purr-fection

This has to be the place. Miss Demeanor is into such off-beat stuff. It's one of the reasons that she still fascinates Mr. Nice Guy; every moment with her is charged with adrenaline, sexuality, and the potential for disaster.

Smoke, pulsing purple light, and chest-compressing bass notes slam against Mr. Nice Guy as he pushes through the door.

A tall, slender man with anemic-white skin stands behind a lectern with a sticker-covered cash box on top. His thick black eyeshadow and wide-lapelled brown suit make him look like a bulimic Count Chocula. He says, "You sure you got the right place, cowboy?"

"Um, pretty sure, yeah," says Mr. Nice Guy.

Count Chocula extends an open palm and says, "Then it's a ten-dollar cover, Mr. Breeder."

Mr. Breeder? Does he think he knows me from somewhere? Maybe I look like one of the regulars.

Mr. Nice Guy hands over two fives and finds a seat near the stage. He glances at his Super G Digital Athletic Chronometer. 11:11 p.m. *Why do they have to start these things so late?* he wonders. Normally, he would be in bed by now.

The atmosphere reminds him of the armpit-and-cheap-cigar-scented strip clubs that Psycho Superstar used to drag him into, but there is also something very different about this place. For one thing, everyone looks like they're attending a Halloween party with prizes for the weirdest and most revealing costumes.

The woman sitting beside him is dressed in a black latex Wendy O. Williams catsuit, with her Betty-and-Veronica-sized silicone breasts rammed into a pair of transparent plastic cones. Her companion is completely naked, save for a pair of tight satin short shorts and red electrical tape *X*s over the nipples of her tiny breasts.

With his orange T-shirt, Levi's jeans, and wide-open mouth, Mr. Nice Guy stands out in this crowd like a nuclear detonation; he only knows about Wendy O. Williams because Miss Demeanor once gave a book report in English class about a volume called *The Wild Women of Punk Rock*. Or something like that.

I do NOT look like one of the regulars.

Both of the strange women frown at Mr. Nice Guy as if the world's biggest zit has just burst in the centre of his forehead.

"Buy a magazine, dude!" the Wendy O. Williams clone barks in a husky voice.

"Or get a hooker!" Electrical-Tape-Nipples grunts.

"Sorry," he says. He didn't mean to stare.

Count Chocula strides out onto the elevated, half-circle stage, and brays, "Ladies and Gentlemen, Butches and Bitches, Pitchers and Catchers and Naughty Children of All Ages, PLEEEEEEeeeeeEEEASE put your HANDS TOGETHER, forRRR … PUSSY … PURRRrrrrRRRRR-FECTION!"

He steps aside, and the noise from the costumed crowd is thunderous as a woman in a cat outfit springs onto the stage on all fours. As she rises to her feet, spiralling like a ballerina to the throbbing music, Mr. Nice Guy realizes that she's not *dressed* as a cat, but her naked body is *painted* like one. His penis extends into the right leg of his Levi's.

Pussy Purr-fection has the sort of long, sinewy legs that Mr. Nice Guy has always admired, and the brown body paint and white leopard spots just accentuate her tapered thighs and angular calf muscles. A burlap tail swings back and forth from her hard round behind, and more cat-spots run along her spine and speckle her muscular back. Triangular cat ears are pinned into her long black hair.

When she spins around, Mr. Nice Guy's eyes fixate on the large white spot painted over her pubic mound, then on the splotches of white over the nipples of her undulating breasts. It takes a moment for him to realize that the face behind the eyeliner-penciled cat whiskers is Miss Demeanor's.

Despite his shock at seeing her onstage, her catlike stretching and clawing causes his shaft to grow even larger, to throb like the pulsing dance music that rattles the room.

She retreats behind the black curtains to wild cheering and applause.

Soon after Count Chocula has returned to announce the next act, Miss Demeanor appears beside Mr. Nice Guy's table. He can see the goosebumps on her skin beneath the brown paint and white spots. Against the cool, smoky air, her whitewashed nipples stick out like .22 calibre bullets, the areolas wrinkled and contracted.

"Hey, buddy," she says. "Thanks for coming."

He glances down at the bulge in the right leg of his jeans. He didn't come, but it was pretty close.

"I half-expected you to bolt before the show even started," she says.

Don't look shocked, he tells himself. *Miss Demeanor loves to shock. Play it cool. Play it cool.*

"Um, nice show, yeah," says Mr. Nice Guy. "Um, the little ears and the tail are nice touches."

"Thanks!" she says. "You should see the flapper outfit I wear for Nostalgia Nights. The hem stops three inches above Hello Kitty."

Hello Kitty is Miss Demeanor's nickname for her genitals. The first and only time that Mr. Nice Guy got a look at Hello Kitty, it was covered over by a triangle of thick, curly pubic hair. It was that one and only glimpse that established Mr. Nice Guy's continuing preference for untrimmed pubes. Now Hello Kitty is as bald as a Mexican Hairless.

"Listen," she says, wrinking her nose, causing her painted-on whiskers twitch, "It's freezing in here. My nipples are about to freakin' *shatter*."

He would like to offer to warm them with his hands, but Mr. Nice Guy would never say something like that. That's the sort of thing that Jake would do, not him. He just nods in an understanding way.

"I'm just going to pop into the back and change into my street clothes, okay? I won't be long. Enjoy the show in the meantime."

*

Mr. Nice Guy's penis stands down from Red Alert Mode during Dame Edna Leathertongue's performance; there is something disturbing to him about the aggression in her military-themed burlesque, although Electrical-Tape-Nipples and Wendy O. Williams seem to enjoy it.

Mr. Nice Guy's blood flows south once again, though, when Marilinn Munrow strides onto the stage. She steps over a fan mounted on the floor, and his jaw drops as her skirt blows up to reveal a thick brown bush.

Right, thinks Mr. Nice Guy, *Marilyn Monroe was really a brunette. Now* that's *attention to detail.*

Unlike the real Marilyn, though, Ms. Munrow is in no hurry to push the fluttering skirt back down again. Mr. Nice Guy applauds enthusiastically.

The Wendy O. Williams clone rolls her eyes at him and says, "Don't get too excited, buddy. It's a merkin."

"What?" Mr. Nice Guy shouts over the pounding music. "American?"

Jeez, I know that Marilyn Monroe was American. And her name was really Norma Jean.

"A *merkin*," Wendy O. says slowly. "A. Mer. Kin."

"Um, ahh … okay. Yeah. Thanks."

Wendy O. rolls her eyes again, and elbows Electrical-Tape-Nipples, who shakes her head.

Mr. Nice Guy worries that maybe he's been staring at Ms. Munrow's hirsute crotch for an impolite amount of time when a bouncer with a dyed-blue Mowhawk appears from behind the stage and strides directly toward him. His eyes fixate on the lean biceps flexing beneath the blue-green tattoos, and only when the bouncer is a few paces from Mr. Nice Guy's table does he notice the breasts swaying beneath the black muscle shirt.

"Hey, thanks for waiting," Miss Demeanor says as she

pulls up a chair beside him. "That body paint takes forever to wash off."

The flash of a stage strobe reveals that there are still traces of eyeliner-pencil whiskers on her cheeks. Faint streaks of white makeup remain overtop the tattoos on her arms. She didn't have any tattoos the last time he saw her, except for the little Chinese symbol on her wrist, an over-publicized high-school graduation gift from Psycho Superstar. Now her shoulders and arms are covered in rose vines and barbed wire, which wind their way past a pink triangle, a yin-yang symbol, an Irish rose, a Wiccan pentacle, portraits of Betty Boop and Bettie Page.

"So," she says, running her fingers through the strip of spiked blue hair that divides her otherwise bald skull, "I guess you've pieced everything together, huh?"

"Umm, yeah," he says. "Yeah. For sure."

"Good. I'm glad you're not freaking out about it. I'll tell the others at your cottage on the long weekend, when the right moment presents itself. But I wanted you to know first." She draws circles on the tabletop with her fingernail. "I was worried that maybe you wouldn't understand. But you're cool? Everything's cool?"

"So, um, you're an exotic dancer. Um, sure, yeah. That's totally cool with me. I can totally live with that. Yeah."

"That's not exactly what I mean, pal."

"Oh, you mean the tattoos. The haircut? Um, well, sure. The new look suits you. Very daring, yeah."

Miss Demeanor sighs. "You see Marilinn Munrow up there, buddy? She's gay. She's a lesbian."

"I don't mind," Mr. Nice Guy says, grinning.

"Dame Edna Leathertongue? She's a butch."

"Yeah, I agree," Mr. Nice Guy confides. "Her show was a bit, um, aggressive for my tastes. It was a bit of a turn-off."

Miss Demeanor sighs again. This is going to be more difficult than she thought. She tilts her head toward Wendy O. Williams and Electrical-Tape-Nipples.

"See those two women? They aren't women, buddy. They're men. Men who *want* to be women."

Mr. Nice Guy's mouth opens slowly, wide enough that Miss Demeanor can see his tonsils.

"Like me," she says, "only vice-versa."

Miss Demeanor can see Mr. Nice Guy's tonsils now.

"Understand?"

Mr. Nice Guy blinks. "You, *umm* … you … are you saying that you … *ummmm* . . . want to be a *man*?"

She laughs. "No, buddy, no. I like my lady bits just the way they are. I *love* 'em, as a matter of fact. They bring me lots of pleasure. And I love other ladies' lady bits, too, if you know what I mean."

Mr. Nice Guy just blinks. "I'm attracted to women, dude. Just as much as you are. Maybe more so." Miss Demeanor punches him lightly on the shoulder. "Just kidding, sport."

Mr. Nice Guy blinks again. Is he missing the point *intentionally?*

"I'm gay, buddy. I'm gay."

"When?" he finally says. "When did you know?"

"I've always known, really."

"But what about you and Jake? What about all those other guys? What about …"

He stops himself. He can't say it.

What about that one time with me? Lying there on the beach under the full moon? With me stretched out beside you? And your shirt rolled up and my hands on your breasts?

You left blood-red lipstick prints all over my face and neck and chest.

I kissed my way down from your face to your stomach, and then I pushed up that red miniskirt, I pulled down those black lace panties, and I went places I'd never gone before.

With you. I went there with you.

Even with the mohawk and the tattoos and the clothes like a small-town auto mechanic's, Miss Demeanor is still beautiful to Mr. Nice Guy. He still sees her long hair shimmering black as crow feathers, brushing her bare shoulders as she lies back on the pebbles. He still feels the warm softness of her breasts in his hands. He still feels the tickle of her pubic hair against his nose and chin. He still wants her.

What about that night? What about that night with me?

Miss Demeanor reads his face and sighs again. Poor Mr. Nice Guy. She should have expected this.

"Buddy," she says, "never underestimate the power of denial."

THE STATISTICIAN

"When you get a little older, you'll see how easy it is to become lured by the female of the species."

— BATMAN, TO ROBIN, FROM THE TV SERIES *BATMAN*, 1966–1968

A.K.A.: Professor G, The Android

SEX: Male **HEIGHT:** 5'11" **WEIGHT:** 195 pounds

CIVILIAN ROLE: Associate Professor, University of Toronto

SPECIAL POWERS: Mathematics. Hyper-rationality.

SPECIAL EQUIPMENT:
His Special Equipment rarely gets used.

SPECIAL VEHICLES:
His own two feet.
Or, when he is in a hurry, the Toronto Transit
Commission's Yonge subway line.
Or, when he absolutely has to, Time Bomb's obnoxious
Cadillac Escalade SUV.

FAVOURED ELIXIRS: British beer. Single-malt Scotch.

SLOGAN/MANTRA: "The numbers never lie."

THE INDIFFERENCE LEAGUE

DID YOU KNOW?
The Statistician has never lost a game of Monopoly, nor
the military strategy game Risk, even when playing against
Royal Military College graduate SuperKen, who claims
that The Statistician is "just lucky." The Statistician does
not believe in luck.

The Statistician walks away from his campus office and toward the undergraduate student ghetto. There is a slight, uncharacteristic swagger in his measured pace. He runs through the numbers in his head:

The number of times that my wife and I have had sex in the past year: 7.

Expressed as a fraction of the total number of days in the year: 7/365.

He does a quick calculation.

A success rate of 1.9 percent.

Abysmal.

But, okay, The Statistician thinks, *perhaps I'm biasing the numbers somewhat. Let's be realistic about it. Subtracting the number of days we can't have sex because of her menstrual cycle, or because one or the other of us is sick or otherwise incapacitated, let's say one week out of every four ...*

He frowns.

7/280. 2.5 percent.

Abysmal, indeed.

And The Statistician is not even using the narrow Bill Clinton definition of sex; in addition to penetrative intercourse, his figure includes manual and/or oral stimulation of the genitals by a sexual partner.

He sighs. The average married couple in his demographic bracket has sex together 2.5 times per week; Mr. And Mrs. Average get it on more times in one month than he and his wife do in an entire *year*. But there is something else, another set of numbers that he finds particularly difficult to reconcile.

The number of times I've stimulated my wife orally during our sexual encounters in the past year (expressed as a fraction): 7/7.

The number of times she's stimulated me orally during the same sexual encounters (expressed as a fraction): 0/7.

The number of times I've brought her to orgasm through oral stimulation during our nine-year marriage: 150 (estimated).

The number of times she's given me oral sex during our entire nine-year marriage: 2 (exact number).

The first time was on their wedding night. She had tried to swallow his ejaculate, but she ran squealing into the hotel-room lavatory to spit it in the sink. Before they could continue consummating their marriage, she had to guzzle down two full glasses of champagne "to get rid of the taste."

The Statistician found this episode puzzling, since at least three of his former girlfriends had described his cum as tasting "sweet"; one even habitually "helped herself to some protein" as he drove her over to Sunday brunch with her parents. This particular girlfriend would then kiss her mother and father right on the lips as soon as she stepped into their pancake-and-bacon-scented home.

The Statistician's wife tried again a couple of nights later, but she gagged violently a few seconds into the process, mascara-blackened tears streaming down her face. He didn't mind the interruption much, though, since she immediately shrugged her lacy teddy onto the marble floor of the honeymoon suite, slipped into her tallest high-heels, then clip-clopped across the room and slowly bent over in front of the brass-studded ottoman, resting her elbows on the cool black leather.

The perfection of my wife's ass during our honeymoon, in comparison to all the other pairs of buttocks in the world, expressed as a percent: 90 percent.

How sexually excited I was by the vision of her in that position, with that upside-down-heart shaped ass up in the air and her long hair flowing over the ottoman and onto the floor, expressed as a percent (with one 100 percent representing orgasm-level excitement): 96 percent.

The Statistician encircled her small waist in his hands, and was able to complete eleven thrusts before exploding inside of her. He couldn't quite make it to an even dozen, let alone the triple digits to which he normally aspired. She just looked too good. It just felt too good.

*

The number of days after our honeymoon ended that she had her hair cut into its current shoulder-length bob: 3.

The relative perfection of my wife's ass, present day, in comparison to all the other pairs of buttocks in the world, expressed as a percent: still 90 percent.

Number of times my wife has assumed that enticing standing-bottoms-up position since our honeymoon: 0.

Number of times my wife has performed fellatio on me since our honeymoon: 0.

Every month for a year after their wedding, when his wife wouldn't let him come inside her because of her period or whatever other reason, The Statistician would suggest that perhaps she could please maybe (please!) consider trying to give him another blow job. She would consistently respond that it wasn't nice to *ask* for such things, that it was more gentlemanly to wait until they were *offered*.

Then she would roll over in bed, turning her back to him, a manoeuvre meant to convey her disappointment and disinterest. However, this also meant that her ninetieth-percentile ass was aimed in his direction all night, and The Statistician's resulting erection would keep him awake until sunrise.

Now every night she sleeps with her back turned to him. It's not a punishment anymore, just a habit.

Number of times in the past year I've had to get out of bed and sneak barefoot across the cold tile floor into the en suite bathroom, to stand on my tiptoes in front of the clamshell-shaped sink, imagining that my wife is bent over in front me, that my lotion-filled fist is her upturned vagina, just to relieve the tension enough that I can get a couple hours of sleep: 40 (estimated).

Number of times in the past year that I've performed a similar operation in front of the sink, imagining that my lotion-filled fist is her mouth instead: 60 (estimated).

*

The Statistician eventually stopped asking his wife for oral sex, but of course he didn't stop wanting it. Last year, in the car on their annual trip to Mr. Nice Guy's cottage, he asked her if maybe she found him less attractive than she used to. She just kissed his neck and smiled.

His brain knew that he should leave this tender moment alone, but his penis still wanted answers.

"If you're indeed still attracted to me, then how come you never …"

She knew where this was going before he even finished the sentence. She sighed, "Look, sweetie, one of these days I'll try again. When I'm ready, okay? My mouth is pretty small, and, well, your thing is pretty big."

She could never call it a cock, a dick, a rod, or a prick. She could barely even refer to it as a penis, and that was only when she was speaking in clinical terms ("What are those abrasions on your penis?" or "Change your pants. I can see your penis through the ones you're wearing"). Otherwise, she always called it his "thing."

"Getting my hand around it is difficult enough, never mind my mouth," she said, shrugging her small shoulders. "It's enormous, really."

Well! That made the Statistician feel pretty good. He'd measured it with a carpenter's ruler once (never mind why he had an erection while trimming a piece of shelving), and, regardless of whose calculation of average one compared it to, he knew that his cock was, statistically speaking, certainly longer and thicker than average. But, *enormous?* Well!

But later at Mr. Nice Guy's cottage, he watched his wife eat a whole cucumber, and then a banana, and The Statistician was pretty sure that his penis wasn't bigger than either of those things.

*

The Statistician double-checks the note cupped in his sweaty left palm. In neat, girly script, the pink paper reads:

> Your Protégée!
> 135 Cheapside Ave
> Apartment C
> C U L8R!!!

He hesitates for a moment on the broken concrete steps of this former upper-middle-class brownstone, which has been converted into bachelor apartments for students who can't afford to live in the university residences.

Number of book club meetings my wife has attended in the past year compared to the number of times she's had sex with me, expressed as a ratio: 24:7.

Number of sex acts my wife has read about in the "literary romance novels" selected by her book club in the past year (calculation based on an assumed average 4 sex acts per book), compared to the number of times she's had actual sex with me in the past year, expressed as a ratio: 96:7.

Number of times in the past year that she has opened her legs for Pedro (the esthetician who trims and waxes her pubic hair) compared to the number of times she's opened her legs me, expressed as a ratio: 26:7.

For some reason, this figure in particular disturbs him the most. She goes to such pains, every two weeks and at no small expense, to have the entrance manicured so invitingly, and yet, as soon as he catches a glimpse of her neatly trimmed pubis and it has the desired effect on him, she closes the gates.

The Statistician presses the buzzer button for Apartment C. He shifts from side to side for a few minutes, waiting, perspiring. He is about to turn away when The Protégé peeks out through the mail slot, and then the door swings open.

"Hey there, Professor," she says. "Thanks for coming."

She's wearing a tight white tank top with no bra underneath. Her breasts retain close to 100 percent of their youthful firmness, forming nearly mathematically-perfect half-spheres, her nipples just a few degrees north of perfect centre. Judging from the coy language she used in his office this afternoon, and from the way she dipped her eyelashes and flicked her upper lip with the tip of her tongue after each sentence, The Statistician estimates that the probability of seeing her naked breasts today is perhaps about 66.7 percent, and her entire unclothed body, approximately 33.3 percent.

The Statistician reassures himself: *It is okay for me to do this. It's justified.*

He follows her up the creaky, round-edged stairs, watching her muscular buttocks flex beneath her clingy red miniskirt. She's got an altogether different type of ass than his wife's, a smaller waist-to-hip ratio to be sure, a bit less cushion perhaps, rounder, firmer. Equally nice, though; another ninetieth-percentile butt. The Statistician's heart rate increases from 80 to 130 beats per minute, and it isn't just from climbing to the top of the stairs.

It's okay for me to do this.

The Protégée pushes open the door to her cluttered, claustrophobic bachelor apartment, which was likely nothing more than a walk-in closet during the building's previous life as a single-family home. Inside, they sit down together on the lone piece of furniture, a rumpled futon bed. Between her slightly parted knees, he glimpses her stop-light-yellow panties. *Proceed with Caution. Prepare to Stop.*

It's justified, he tells himself again.

"So," The Protégée says, opening a notebook filled with complex arithmetical scribbling, "like I mentioned in your office, I've really been having some difficulty making sense of these numbers."

Her fingers brush his forearm as she flips the next page of her calculations open before him. Her thigh presses against his. She looks at him with big liquid eyes, her head titled slightly to one side, her lashes gently dropping at regular intervals. It's the same way his wife used to look at him around the time they got engaged. Before she cut her hair. Before the book club. Before Pedro the Esthetician. Before she started sleeping with her back to him. Before the numbers tapered off to seven times a year.

"The numbers never lie," says The Statistician to The Protégée.

TIME BOMB

"You mean to tell me you've been married to her for fifteen years? And they call me Superman!"

— SUPERMAN, TO RICKY RICARDO, FROM THE
TV SERIES *I LOVE LUCY*, 1951–1957

SUPERHERO PROFILE: TIME BOMB

A.K.A.: "That Bitch" (especially by shop clerks, domestic employees, and bistro waitresses)

SEX: Female **HEIGHT:** 5'2" **WEIGHT:** 105 pounds

CIVILIAN ROLE: Consumer

SPECIAL POWERS: Can shoot Daggers of Ice from her eyes (metaphorically speaking).

SPECIAL EQUIPMENT: Her Holt Renfrew wardrobe and her Stairmaster-Toned, Multiple-Personal-Trainer-Enhanced physique make Time Bomb intimidating to enemies (usually retail-store clerks), despite her diminutive size.

SPECIAL VEHICLES: An "empowering" black Cadillac Escalade SUV.

FAVOURED ELIXIRS:
Champagne (Breakfast), Chardonnay (Lunch), Martinis (Evenings); must be chilled to exactly the right temperature, or the drink goes back and you forfeit your tip.

SLOGAN/MANTRA: *"Ah-shee! Ah-shee! Ah-SHAH!"*

THE INDIFFERENCE LEAGUE

DID YOU KNOW?
Due to her "respiratory and dermatological sensitivities," Time Bomb sleeps on a special hypoallergenic pillow; her housekeeper replaces the nine-hundred-dollar pillow once per month. Fortunately, the annual interest from her trust fund is more than ten times the employment income of any other member of The Indifference League.

Time Bomb reaches out and slaps the Snooze button on the digital alarm clock beside their bed for the fourth time. "Ten more minutes," she moans, turning over on her side.

Beside her, The Statistician stirs. He sidles over to her, puts one arm around her waist. Soon she feels his erection poking into the softness of her behind, like she's hiding in a utility closet and has backed into a broom handle. How romantic.

"Aw, honey," she sighs, "not this morning, okay?"

The same response as yesterday, thinks The Statistician. *And the day before that. And the fifty-six days before that. One more day, and we will have set a new personal record for marital abstinence.*

He slips out from under the duvet and plods into the en suite, his erection bobbing before him like the prow of a sailing vessel. When he closes the door behind him, she knows he's going in there to jerk off into the bathroom sink. He leaves the door wide open when he's brushing his teeth, showering, or using the toilet, but masturbation is still private business for The Statistician.

This is okay with Time Bomb; it means she has a few minutes to herself. She rolls over onto her back, spreads her legs wide, and begins turning slow circles with her middle finger. As her finger spins faster, pushes down harder, she is not thinking about The Statistician. Just like when he goes down on her, she is thinking about someone else.

Before the clamshell-shaped masturbation altar in the en suite, The Statistician is also thinking about someone else. Until a few days ago, he had never fantasized that his lotion-lubricated fist was another woman; he had been faithful to his wife even in his fantasy life. But now he is imagining the slick, rubbery lips of The Protégée sliding up and down on him.

Actually, he isn't imagining so much as *remembering*.

The Statistician can't prevent himself from moaning with both satisfaction and regret as he blasts into the sink. He masks the noise with a few fake coughs, but it doesn't matter anyway, because Time Bomb doesn't hear anything. On the other side of the wall, she is hovering on the edge of an explosion. Her face is flushed, her back is arched, her legs twitch and kick, and she pants like she's running a hundred-yard-dash. At the moment, she wouldn't hear the sound of a bomb falling on their Forest Hill mansion.

The Statistician ambles back into the bedroom, and Time Bomb rolls onto her side, curls up into a fetal-position ball. *So close*, she laments. *So close*.

"Come on, lazybones," The Statistician says, reaching over to pat her bottom. "You'll have to get up if we're going to make it to Mr. Nice Guy's cottage by this afternoon."

"It's Saturday," Time Bomb moans. "I want to sleep in."

"You sleep in every day," The Statistician says.

"Why don't you just go alone?" Time Bomb says, burying her face in her pillow, imagining a whole long weekend to herself.

"Aw, come on, honey," he sighs, "I don't want to go without you."

"Why not? All of them want to see you. None of them want to see me."

The Statistician suspects that this statement is true.

"You know that's not true," he says.

"None of them ever talk to me. They couldn't care less about me."

"SuperBarbie talks to you all the time."

"She's the only one. And the last time, Hippie Avenger tried to kill me!"

"Hey, she felt terrible about that. She grew those flowers herself. She couldn't have known you would react like that."

"She could have asked."

Time Bomb suffers from "respiratory and dermatological sensitivities." Her skin sunburns easily, and she suffers rashes from natural cloth fibres and most grasses. She also has sneezing fits when exposed to cat dander, certain kinds of dust, and most plant pollens. On their last trip to The Hall of Indifference, Hippie Avenger's all-natural flower-oil moisturizing lotion caused Time Bomb a fit of sneezing that forced her to retreat to their bedroom upstairs for the remainder of the night.

Also, Mr. Nice Guy's cologne gave Time Bomb a migraine. She also complains of migraines when it is too hot, too cold, too humid, too dry, too bright, or too noisy.

"You've got a long list of sensitivities, honey," The Statistician says. "It's easy to forget one of them."

"Well, everyone knows that I react to ground pepper, and yet the so-called Mr. Nice Guy had to grind pepper all over everything he cooked. I didn't have anything for dinner last time but a banana and a cucumber."

The Statistician specifically remembers the banana and the cucumber.

"We'll bring a cooler full of food just for you, okay? Some of your tofu burgers, some rye buns, and some raw vegetables. You'll be fine."

Undercooked beef is another of Time Bomb's "migraine triggers," and sometimes commercial wheat buns are brushed with white flour, which makes her sneeze. Time Bomb simply doesn't like the texture of cooked vegetables, and she refuses to eat them.

"I suppose the new blankets Mr. Nice Guy bought are *wool*," she sniffs.

Oh yes. Wool makes Time Bomb's skin break out in hives.

"And he probably bought down-filled pillows." Time Bomb is allergic to goose feathers, too. She sneezes pre-emptively, in her characteristic triplets. *"Ah-shee! Ah-shee! Ah-SHAH!"*

It takes great effort by The Statistician to prevent himself from rolling his eyes or sighing. He estimates that the ratio of the number of his wife's spurious, psychosomatic ailments, compared to the number of actual physical/chemical reactions she suffers, is about 4 to 1.

"We'll bring our own blankets," he offers. "And the hypo-allergenic pillows, okay?"

"It would be a lot less trouble if you just went by yourself," she says.

Indeed, the Statistician thinks to himself, *it* would *be a lot less trouble*. He is very careful to ensure that his facial expression does not betray this thought, though.

Yesterday, The Statistician merely raised an eyebrow when Time Bomb mispronounced every other syllable in the phrase "unequivocally effete" over champagne and chèvre-on-toast with her favourite shopping/manicure/lunch buddy, and Time Bomb countered with a "joke" that they would be still be eating Kraft Dinner and sipping Budweiser from plastic cups if they had to rely solely on The Statistician's income.

"Thank God for my trust fund!" said Time Bomb.

Her father is the CEO of a large tobacco company, the one famous for commissioning and publishing its own "independent medical studies" that "prove" smoking is as good for a person's health as eating an apple or taking a brisk autumn walk. Time Bomb's daddy does not smoke cigarettes, but he drinks enough Scotch to power the crew of a British battleship.

"Thank God your father made him sign a pre-nup!" Spa Buddy giggled.

After Spa Buddy went home, The Statistician angrily offered to resign his position as an untenured junior professor, to pursue a less academically stimulating, but more lucrative job crunching numbers in the private sector.

Time Bomb's response was to shrug and scoff, "What difference do you think an extra twenty grand a year will make in *this* neighbourhood? At least being a professor *sounds* respectable." She slugged back the last of the champagne and said, "Don't make me look stupid, and I won't make you sound worthless. Fair enough?"

The Statistician is not eager for a replay of this conversation in front of his friends at Mr. Nice Guy's cottage, so he will carefully regulate his facial expressions around his wife for the time being.

"Hey," The Statistician says, smiling, squeezing Time Bomb's shoulder, "my brother will be there."

For some reason, Time Bomb is quite fond of The Drifter.

"Will we get to meet his new girlfriend?" she asks, her countenance brightening.

"Yes, he's bringing her along. Apparently she's quite a stunner."

"Oh, okay, fine," Time Bomb says, finally sitting up in bed. "I'll go. But I bet I won't have any fun."

That, thinks The Statistician, *is a safe bet, indeed.*

THE STUNNER

*"No one can resist the golden lasso.
It binds all who are encircled …"*

— WONDER WOMAN, FROM THE TV SERIES
WONDER WOMAN, 1975–1979

SUPERHERO PROFILE: THE STUNNER

A.K.A.: Honey, Sweetie, Beautiful, Hottie, Sexy, Baby

SEX: Female **HEIGHT:** 5'7" **WEIGHT:** 130 pounds

CIVILIAN ROLE: Student, University of Toronto

SPECIAL POWERS:
Academically brilliant.
Magnetically attractive to men.

SPECIAL VEHICLES:
Men who drive Mercedes and BMWs seem to be
especially generous.

FAVOURED ELIXIRS:
Formerly: Domestic beer.
Currently: French wines and fine coffees.

SLOGANS/MANTRAS:
The Chorus to the U2 song "I Still Haven't Found What
I'm Looking For" plays frequently on The Stunner's
mental soundtrack.

THE INDIFFERENCE LEAGUE

DID YOU KNOW?
Every single boy (including the gay one) at The Stunner's
high school fantasized about taking her to the Senior Prom.
Even a couple of her teachers thought about asking her.
None of them did, though, so on Prom Night The Stunner
just stayed home and watched *Dirty Dancing* again on TV.

The Stunner was magnetically attractive to men, especially older men, from a fairly early age, but she didn't become fully aware of her powers until the night before she went away to university in Toronto.

Because she spent her first eighteen years living with her parents in a Northern Ontario copper-mining town, The Stunner breezily dismissed the frequent advances toward her as a function of the town's twenty-to-one male-to-female ratio. When the men's shifts in the mine ended on payday, there wasn't much else for them to do but go out drinking, and certainly all that Labatt 50 and Molson Export didn't clarify their perception of an early-blossoming girl's age relative to their own.

During her last summer up North, when she tended the bar at the Rockslide Pub, the men often left behind exorbitant 100-percent tips for her. When she worked the odd shift at the curling-rink snack bar, the grinning old-timers usually told her to "*Keep the change, beautiful,*" when they handed her a ten or a twenty for a bag of stale mixed nuts. Yet, The Stunner didn't suspect that she was being treated any differently than any other girl in town.

Then, on her last Saturday night working the bar at the Rockslide, just hours before she would catch a ride in Red Brown's Piper Cub to Thunder Bay to board her flight to Toronto, The Stunner heard a confession that changed everything. She was pouring another pint for Eddie Jansen, who was only five years older than The Stunner, and already a foreman at the copper mine. Eddie was pretty cute, and she had felt a friction between them ever since he came to town, but he had never once made a pass at her. She decided to ask him why. What did she have to lose?

Eddie's already glassy eyes filled with tears. "Aw my Gawd," he said, "Aw my Gawd. If only I'd known, Gawd … I would have …"

"You would have what, Eddie?"

"Aw, I couldn't have, anyway. Nobody could."

"Huh? What are you talking about?"

"You're … you're *untouchable*."

"*Untouchable*? What? Come on, Eddie! I don't have cooties."

"Aw, it's, it's not that. It's …"

"I'm not stuck-up. I'm not a prude. I've always been nice to you, haven't I? I've never pushed you away."

"Nope. You sure haven't."

"And I'm not the worst-looking girl in town."

"Gawd no. Gawd no. You're the … every man in town wants you. *Every* man."

"Eddie, I really don't care about the other men. But I've always kind of liked *you*."

"Aw, Gawd, yeah. I know."

"Well, then? How come you never …?"

"It's your father," he blurts.

"My father?"

"He scares the shit outta me. He scares the shit outta *everyone*."

"But … how do you know my father? He never comes in here."

"He doesn't come in while you're *here*. He always shows up about a half an hour before your shift starts. He'll walk up to a guy randomly, and say, 'You know that little cutie who works the late shift here?' And when the guy nods approvingly, he'll point to his big hunting boots, and say something like, 'Well, she's my daughter, and if you so much as look at her the wrong way, these boots will crush your skull and stomp your eyes out.' Or he'll pick up a pool cue, point it at the guy, and say, 'This is where I'll be aiming my Remington thirty-aught-six if you ever touch her. Hollow-point bullets. Big exit wound, oh yeah.' And it's not just the young guys; sometimes he puts on this same show for the old geezers who haven't had a boner in twenty years."

The Stunner's father was one of the biggest in a town full of big men, but she always thought of him as a cuddly, overstuffed teddy bear; she knew he could put on an intimidating act when he needed to, but she had never imagined anything like this. She wasn't sure whether to be grateful for his protection, or angry that he'd meddled in her life this way.

She leaned on her elbows on the bar, and Eddie couldn't help stealing a look through the open collar of her blouse.

"How about tonight, Eddie?" she cooed. "It'll be your last chance, sweetie. I'm leaving for university tomorrow morning."

"Aww, geez," Eddie moaned, twisting from side to side on his bar stool. "I'd give my entire life's savings for just one night with you, I really would. Any man in the whole friggin' town would." He gulped down the last dregs of his beer, his Adam's apple bobbing. "I'm not sure I'm ready to die for it, though."

And with that said, Eddie Jansen emptied all the cash from his wallet onto the top of the bar, and slid from his stool, muttering, "Good luck at college, eh?" He slunk out of the Rockslide Pub with his hands jammed into the pockets of his work pants.

The Stunner's brain arranged and processed these new facts. She was a smart girl, by far the best student in the town's under-populated high school. She'd brought the average of her entire advanced mathematics class up to the provincial standard by earning 99 percent on her final exam (and she had cried over that lost 1 percent). She'd earned an entrance scholarship to the University of Toronto. So she was smart.

And she was attractive, too, much more so than she had imagined just a few moments earlier.

And her brain told her body what she needed to do next.

She undid a button on her blouse.

Her conscience cried out: *What if your father walks in?*

She undid another button.

What if he does? Tomorrow I'll be gone.

Then she hiked her skirt up as high as it would go, exposing more of her tapered thighs than the patrons of the Rockslide Pub had ever seen before, or would ever see again.

"It's my last night in town, boys!" she hollered. "Everybody's next beer is on me!"

Of course none of the men let her pay for their drinks, and the next morning The Stunner stepped out of Red Brown's Piper Cub onto the runway in Thunder Bay with her purse full of cash tips almost equal to the copper mine's weekly payroll.

*

Since then, The Stunner has rarely ever paid for a restaurant meal or a drink in a bar. Some drooling, horny boy or desperate, greying mid-lifer will always cover her tab in exchange for a few hours of her attention. All she has to do is nod, smile, giggle occasionally, suggest vaguely that they might get to see her naked body later, and men will empty their wallets in exchange for anything she desires.

Two years earlier, her idea of a Big Night Out was a quarter-chicken dinner and a couple of bottles of Labatt Blue at the Swiss Chalet near the mine site, but since her father isn't around Toronto to point at his hunting boots and shake pool cues in men's faces, she's developed a connoisseur's appreciation for French wines, fine coffees, fresh oysters, and *fois gras*. All it takes is a high-hemmed skirt and a low-collared sweater.

And the blowjob! It has become the nuclear warhead in her arsenal; so easy to deploy, so massive in its impact. Giving head is as easy as enjoying a vanilla Popsicle, but it doesn't take nearly as long to finish. And afterward, the recipient is your slave for as long as you want him to be. Just promise him another. Soon! Very soon!

If she'd known about the blowjob when she was still in Northern Ontario, she could have been the richest ex-barmaid at the University of Toronto. Still, it is a skill that has served her well in the short time she's had to master it. And she enjoys doing it. She loves the feelings of power and control as they moan and spasm and twitch with every slight manoeuvre. It's a win-win situation for everyone involved.

*

So, the Stunner is magnetically attractive to men. It's like a superpower, and so far she's only used it in small doses. There are untapped reserves of Potential Energy crackling deep inside her, though, and as soon as she meets a truly Worthy Man, she will let herself go Kinetic on him.

THE DRIFTER

"Clark *is who I am.* Superman *is what I can do.*"

— CLARK KENT (A.K.A. SUPERMAN), FROM THE
TV SERIES *SMALLVILLE*, 2001–2011

SUPERHERO PROFILE: THE DRIFTER

A.K.A.: Little Brother

SEX: Male **HEIGHT:** 5'11" **WEIGHT:** 185 pounds

CIVILIAN ROLE: Between jobs

SPECIAL POWERS:
Clark Kent/Superman transformation.

SPECIAL EQUIPMENT:
Black motorcycle helmet. Black leather jacket.

SPECIAL VEHICLES:
1968 Norton Commando motorcycle.

FAVOURED ELIXIRS:
British beer. Single-malt Scotch. The Stunner's coffee.

SLOGAN/MANTRA:
"Keep moving."

THE INDIFFERENCE LEAGUE

DID YOU KNOW?
The Drifter is the only member of The Indifference League to ever beat The Statistician at poker. Although The Statistician claims to play "only mathematically, never emotionally," and that he hence cannot be "read," The Drifter has always been able to tell when The Statistician is bluffing.

he Drifter cranks back the handgrip, and the big air-cooled engine of his 1968 Norton Commando responds with a roar. There is no hesitation or sputtering; his most recent tune-up effort has been successful. He grins behind the helmet's face-shield.

Accelerating into one of the long, sloping curves so common in this part of the country, he grips the gas tank between his knees and leans with the bike like it's an extension of his body. His passenger shifts awkwardly on the seat behind him, and he automatically compensates, keeping the turn smooth and even.

It occurs to him that carrying a passenger on a motor-cycle is a lot like sustaining an intimate relationship; when one person makes a move that threatens to unbalance the ride, the other has to make a counter-move to keep things going, to prevent the crash. Since meandering through Europe and Asia atop the old Norton, lovingly tuning and repairing it along the way, The Drifter has seen metaphors and analogies everywhere while gripping its vibrating handlebars.

The road straightens ahead of them and the bike rights itself. The Drifter's passenger tightens her grip around his chest, clenches his hips between her thighs, pulls her chest tight against his back. The Drifter relishes the contact, believing that he can see their future in the tarmac that streaks toward them.

His passenger is living only in the present, closing her eyes and enjoying her unexpected physical reaction to the perfect frequency of the vibration between her legs.

He calls out to her over the rumble of the engine, "We're almost there!"

She certainly is.

*

She had felt a similar tingling when she met The Drifter for the first time at that cheap Chinese noodle joint on Spadina. She'd been sitting alone atop a tall stool facing the rain-streaked window, dwelling on something she'd just done that she wished she hadn't. She had just given herself permission to cry about it when The Drifter appeared beside her, his black motorcycle helmet in one hand, a cardboard container of steaming rice noodles in the other.

"Is this spot taken?" he asked in that raspy voice, nodding at the empty stool beside her.

"It is now," she replied, trying to sound less pathetic than she felt.

His battered leather jacket was speckled with beads of rain, and strands of wet hair were plastered across his forehead like the tributaries of a deep, black river.

They both ate in silence, until she mustered the nerve to say something.

"Looking for some shelter from the weather?"

"I don't mind the rain," he said.

He didn't. This storm was a mere spring shower compared to some of the monsoon downpours in Southeast Asia. On his journey to see Angkor Wat in Cambodia, so much water poured from the sky that it knocked him right off the bike. The road became a rushing, muddy river, and he could do nothing but lie there and grip the Norton's handlebars to keep from being swept away. It was like being towed behind a speedboat.

He held on tight, and, for the first time in his life, he prayed. He still isn't sure whose version of God he was reaching out to, but he prayed intensely and sincerely that his life might continue after the deluge. It did. And The Drifter was grateful.

"Little changes in the weather don't bother me much anymore," The Drifter said, shaking a droplet of rain from the end of his nose. "I was just hungry for some noodles."

Her heart beat faster. Her cheeks flushed hot. *Don't be an idiot*, she told herself. *There is no such thing as love at first sight.*

After they had both finished eating, and they'd made all the small talk that can be made before moving on to bigger topics or just moving on, she asked him, "So … do you live around here?"

"For the moment I do."

He had just moved into one of the U of T student residences. They rented them out during the summer months, when most of the undergraduates went back to their hometowns. The Drifter's older brother, an associate professor, had made the arrangements for the dorm room, and even paid the security deposit, which was the sort of thing that made him feel Big Brotherly and In Control of Things. For The Drifter, suffering some mild condescension from The Statistician was fair exchange for a cheap place to stay for a couple of months.

"Want to give me a ride back to my place?" she ventured. "You could come up for a coffee."

"Well, I don't …"

"Seriously, I make great coffee. I make this perfect blend from a nice, earthy single-estate from Southeast Asia, and a dark, fruity roast from South Africa. Warm you right to your bones."

"It sounds great, but I don't …"

"If you don't like coffee, I've got tea, too."

"I'd love a coffee," he said, "but I can't give you a ride on my bike. I don't have my extra helmet with me."

"Oh," she said, looking away. "Okay."

When The Drifter saw the dark look in this stranger's eyes reflected back at him from the rain-spotted window, he wanted nothing more than to make her smile, to make her happy, to do whatever she wanted him to do.

"But, tell you what," he added, "if you really want to ride in the rain, you can wear mine, okay?"

He stood up and placed his helmet on the counter in front of her. Then he shrugged off his jacket and draped it over her shoulders.

"You should wear this, too. The rain is cold."

She followed him out into the crackling, hissing evening, reminding herself, *There is no such thing as love at first sight.*

*

Given her magnetic power over men, The Stunner was baffled that The Drifter didn't try to steal even a *glimpse* of her naked body as she stripped off her wet clothes. He just sat there on her futon bed and stared at the old iron radiator under the window, over which she had draped his rain-soaked leather jacket. He spoke just once, to say that her coffee was the best he'd ever tasted. He never once looked over his shoulder.

She was about to slip into the lacy little teddy, designed specifically to amplify and focus her magnetic power, but then she felt unusually self-conscious, so she pulled on her comfy fuzzy pajamas instead. Then The Stunner sat cross-legged on the futon beside The Drifter, and asked him, "So why didn't you look at me while I was changing? You're not gay, are you? That would be my luck."

"Um, no. Definitely not. I come from a long line of men with legendary heterosexual libidos. Before birth control, the women in our clan had an average of a dozen children each. I'm amazed that my brother and his wife haven't got five kids already."

He paused to enjoy the rainforest smell of her damp hair, then took another sip of that delicious coffee.

"I *wanted* to watch you undress. Rather *badly*, actually. But you asked me not to. So I didn't."

"Wow," she said. "A real gentleman."

Did that come out sounding sarcastic? She hadn't meant it to.

"If we're going to have a relationship," he said, "I want you to know that you can trust me."

"A relationship?" she scoffed.

She hadn't meant to scoff, either.

"I've travelled a lot of places," he said, "and I've seen a lot of things. And this sort of thing doesn't happen every day."

"What sort of thing? Two people randomly sitting beside each other in a Chinese noodle joint?"

"Nothing in life is random," said The Drifter. "Life brings you exactly what you need, if you let it. The trick is not wanting what you don't need, and recognizing what you need when it shows up."

"Wow. Nice line."

"It's not a line. It's what I believe."

"You can undress me now if you want to," she said, raising her arms in the air so he could more easily lift off her top.

"I'd rather wait."

"You'd rather *wait*? You *are* a *human male*, aren't you?"

"Oh yes," he says, "I *am* a human male. And it hasn't escaped my notice that you have a terrific body."

"I was dressed like a frump at the noodle house, and my pajamas make me look like a monster Muppet. So how do you know I have a *terrific body*? "

"You asked me to look away while you changed your clothes. You didn't say I couldn't watch your reflection in the window."

She felt strangely shy, wanting to burrow under the sheets and hide. At the same time, she wanted him to rip her pajamas off, to ravage her, to lick and kiss her skin, to grab and hold every curve and contour that would fit into his large hands. But she also wanted to just sit here beside him, still and silent, and watch him sip her coffee. She wasn't sure exactly what she wanted, but she knew that she *wanted*.

"The window is pretty dirty. I didn't see much of you," he said. "Just enough."

The polarity of The Stunner's magnetic power flip-flopped from positive to negative to positive to negative to positive again.

"It's not just your body, you know," he finally said. "You have an exquisite face. You have an intoxicating voice. You *smell* fantastic. You are maybe the sexiest woman I've ever met. You are absolutely *stunning*."

Stunning. She liked that. She'd been called *hot, smokin', wicked, sexy, foxy,* and *babe-licious*, but nobody had ever described her as *stunning*. She liked it.

The Drifter drained the last sip of coffee from the mug, quietly, without slurping. She liked that, too.

"This really is the best coffee I've ever had," he said. "And I've had a lot of good coffee in my travels."

Her heart was racing again. Her cheeks were hot.

"Would you like some more?"

"I would."

She carried his cup to the tiny kitchenette, returned it to him full and steaming.

"Tell me about the places you've been," she said.

He did.

He told her about trading two weeks labour knocking down walls in East London for the already-battered Norton Commando, and about all the places it took him from there: Birmingham, Liverpool, Dublin. To Paris, Bordeaux, and Marseilles. Through the Italian Riviera, around the Mediterranean

THE INDIFFERENCE LEAGUE · 83

Sea. Along the Blue Danube, into Prague and Vienna. Past the Black and Caspian and Aral Seas. Through Calcutta, Rangoon, to the Temple of Angkor Wat.

The sound of The Drifter's sandpaper voice scratching over the beautiful names of the places he'd seen made The Stunner want to push him back on the bed and straddle him, ride him until she couldn't stand the pleasure anymore. But she also wanted to close her eyes, hold her breath, and just listen.

He described the frustrations of a dozen mechanical breakdowns, the pain of a hundred acidic growls from his empty stomach, the horror of the flash flood, the delirium of the long, scorching drought, the terror of staring down the barrel of an angry soldier's rifle. He was thankful for it all, even the terrifying parts, the moments when he thought his life was over. *Especially* those parts. Those moments showed him what sort of material he was made of, exactly how much he could withstand if he had to.

"Now tell me about the places you've been," he said.

She did.

Her story took less time to tell, and had fewer stops along the way, but more splendid adjectives. Glints of copper in the steel-grey rocks. Snow banks painted pink by the setting sun. The rippling, ghostly sheets of colour that are the Northern Lights. A thousand little silver lakes viewed through the windows of Cessna and Piper single-props. And then, her recent explorations of the lights and shadows of Toronto at night.

And that was it. That was all she had.

Eventually, the orange light of a new day diffused through the single dusty window.

"Where are you travelling next?" she asked.

"I'm going to ride up to an old friend's cottage next weekend. It's a high-school reunion kind of thing. Want to come?"

As she reminded herself again, *There is no such thing as love at first sight,* she heard herself saying to him, "Yes, I would."

*

As The Drifter eases the Norton Commando though another gentle curve, The Stunner is still telling herself, *There is no such thing as love at first sight. There is no such thing as love at first sight. There is no such thing as love at first sight.*

She closes her eyes, feels the warm wind stroke her body and enjoys the vibration of the engine beneath her.

"Just a few more miles to go," The Drifter calls back to her.

The road straightens again. He twists back the throttle, and the bike surges forward.

Love at first sight. Love at first sight. Love at first sight.

She squeezes the seat between her thighs, and the pure, sustained note that rises from inside her harmonizes with the roar of the engine and the rush of the wind and the rumble of the road beneath her.

Love. Love. Love.

HIPPIE AVENGER

*"Go in peace, my daughter. And remember that, in a
world of ordinary mortals, you are a Wonder Woman."*

— QUEEN HIPPOLYTA, FROM THE TV
SERIES *WONDER WOMAN*, 1975–1979

SUPERHERO PROFILE: HIPPIE AVENGER

A.K.A.: Janis Joplin
(A very stoned young man at a Phish concert kept calling her that, and for a while the nickname stuck.)

SEX: Female **HEIGHT:** 5'6" **WEIGHT:** 140 pounds

CIVILIAN ROLE: Assistant Art Gallery Curator

SPECIAL POWERS: Painting, Sculpting, Writing Poetry, Knitting, Making Candles.

SPECIAL EQUIPMENT:
"The Purple Pal."

SPECIAL VEHICLES:
Late-sixties Volkswagen Microbus.

FAVOURED ELIXIR:
Fair-trade, certified-organic white wine.

SLOGAN/MANTRA:
"One Race: The Human Race."

THE INDIFFERENCE LEAGUE

DID YOU KNOW?
By working at the art gallery, selling her paintings, pottery, scarves, sweaters, and candles, and occasionally babysitting for her landlord, Hippie Avenger makes almost as much money in a year as Time Bomb spends in a month on shoes, clothing, and hypoallergenic pillows.

Hippie Avenger thinks that her Not-So-Super Friend nickname is a bit of a misnomer.

Sure, she still drives the pea-green late-sixties Volkswagen Microbus she inherited from her parents, but it isn't because of any sentimental desire to Keep on Truckin' or be Too Rollin' Stoned, to quote just two of the dozens of bumper stickers permanently affixed the van's exterior. The old Microbus gets her from point A to point B most of the time, and she can't really afford to replace it.

And, sure, she still pulls her long, curly black hair into a ponytail when she doesn't have time to wash and style it, and she still wears the same sort of loose-fitting pastel-coloured smocks and Birkenstock sandals that she's worn since childhood, but none of these things are necessarily symbolic of any great dedication to the idealistic convictions of a bygone era. They are just habits.

And, sure, she doesn't own a cellphone or an MP3 player or a laptop computer or a big-screen TV or any of the other technological devices that seem so important to other people, but it isn't because she is conscientiously boycotting the material trappings of capitalism, nor is she purposely trying to keep money and therefore power out of the hands of the Military-Industrial Complex. She simply doesn't care about any of that stuff. When she is outside her apartment, she doesn't want to listen to digitized music or blather endlessly on the phone, she just wants to look at the trees and listen to the wind (or look at the buildings and listen to the traffic, if that's what happens to be around). She rarely ever checks her email or uses the Internet on her third-hand home computer, so why would she ever need a portable one? And television? When is there anything worthwhile on television?

Her lifestyle choices are not a matter of philosophy; they are merely preferences. Therefore, Hippie Avenger is not a true Hippie. She knows this all too well.

Her parents were genuine tie-dyed, pot-smoking, vegetable-eating, anti-war, anti-establishment, free-lovin', free-wheelin' Hippies. They both turned twenty in 1968, and were already Old Hippies when they finally brought their first and only Love Child into the world ten years later. Now pushing seventy, they are one of the few ragged old couples who still cling to the whole Peace, Love, and Joy thing, and they will still expound at length about the dream of Woodstock, and how it died for most hippies at Altamont, but not for them.

Unlike most other members of their generation, who talk as if they had been there when they really just watched the movies, Hippie Avenger's parents had in fact journeyed to both Woodstock and Altamont, using the money they were supposed to spend on college tuition. They also went to Monterey, and they followed the Grateful Dead for an entire year, all in the same VW Microbus that their Love Child now uses for her weekly trip to the mini-mall to buy the commercial-industrial products that her parents so despise.

Yes, Hippie Avenger sometimes buys manufactured goods from corporate-owned stores. She eats factory-packaged cookies made with unwholesome white flour and sugar refined from cane grown on non-unionized Third-World plantations. She knows that this is philosophically the wrong thing to do, but it's just so much easier than making them from scratch, and they taste uniformly, predictably, okay. She also uses toothpaste manufactured by the same company that made one of the ingredients for Agent Orange during the Vietnam War, because brushing with baking soda like her parents do makes her breath smell like a yeast infection. She even uses disposable razors and commercially produced scented foam to shave her armpits.

Does she feel guilty about doing any of these things? Of course she does. Her parents would be horrified. Her socio-political guilt wages war with her preference for minty freshness every time she brushes her teeth. Whenever she exfoliates under her arms or around her pubic patch, she hears her mother scolding her for "caving in to corporate commercial social norms." If her father knew about his daughter's flagrant use of underarm deodorant, he would launch into a tirade about how "the minions of commercialism have spent millions of advertising dollars to make us fear the scent of our own humanity."

And yet, still she eats Chips Ahoy! cookies, brushes with Crest, exfoliates with Gillette, and masks the scent of her humanity with Lady Speed Stick. She knows that she really isn't a hippie at all. She only sort of looks like one. So her nickname, Hippie Avenger, is not quite right. But so far nobody has come up with anything better.

She sighs as she heaves a burlap bag into the back of the Microbus, which contains a couple changes of clothes, her toothbrush, hairbrush, razor, and the only portable, battery-powered technology she owns: a purple, plastic-and-rubber, quasi-penis-shaped vibrator. Of course she would rather feel a real, organic penis moving inside her, and of course she would prefer the tongue of a real man flicking at her sensitive clitoris, but in the meantime she's grown quite fond of her Purple Pal. Certainly it brings her more pleasure than a TV, a cellphone or a laptop computer ever could.

The Orgasm is one of the few luxuries that Hippie Avenger was taught not to feel guilty about wanting. She considers slipping back inside her apartment for a quick self-pleasuring session, but she's already an hour behind schedule. She is always running late, probably the result of growing up in a home free from the tyranny of clocks.

She climbs up into the driver's seat of the Microbus, wondering if she's remembered to unplug the coffee percolator, or to lock the door to her apartment above the detached, bungalow-sized garage of her landlord's suburban stucco-covered-cardboard McMansion. She shrugs. If her place gets robbed or burns down it won't make any difference to her; she doesn't own anything of real value, either monetary or sentimental. It's one of the few old bumper stickers on the VW that actually reflects her own feelings: THINGS ARE JUST NOT MY THING.

Hippie Avenger slides the key into the ignition on the scratched-up steering column and turns it. Nothing happens. She wiggles the key and tries again. Still nothing. Then she notices that the switch for the headlights is pulled out.

Damn it! I left the lights on again.

She walks around to the front of the McMansion. Her landlord and his wife have already departed for the holiday weekend, so she won't be able to beg for yet another jump-start.

Great. Like, now what am I going to do?

Hippie Avenger doesn't feel comfortable approaching one of her neighbours for help, because she still hasn't met any of them (typical of these soulless, anti-community, commuter-culture subdivisions, her parents would be quick to point out). Besides, she doesn't actually know how to open the engine compartment on the Microbus, or where to connect the clamps on the ends of the tangled jumper cables. It's her landlord who always jump starts her van, and she has never paid much attention to how he does it. He is an expert on the mechanics of lawn mowers and weed trimmers and gas grills and other suburban gadgets that might as well be sub-molecular-particle accelerators as far as Hippie Avenger is concerned.

She climbs the stairs to her garage-top apartment. She has, in fact, left the door unlocked. In the kitchen, she switches off the coffee percolator, reaches for the telephone, and dials Mr. Nice Guy's number. He won't mind swinging through Guelph to give her a ride to The Hall of Indifference; that's why they call him Mr. Nice Guy. She gets his voice mail, though; he's probably en route to the cottage already, and law-abiding, safety-conscious Mr. Nice Guy would never talk on his cellphone while driving.

Next she tries Miss Demeanor; a recorded message informs her that "The caller you are trying to reach is currently unavailable," which means that Miss Demeanor is probably engaged in another war of attrition with her cell service provider.

Hippie Avenger doesn't have a current number for The Drifter, so there is really only one other choice. She hesitates before dialling.

Maybe she should just stay home for the weekend. Of the eight original Not-So-Super Friends, Hippie Avenger and The Statistician have the least in common. They probably wouldn't be friends at all if not for the others. It might actually be less unpleasant for Hippie Avenger to spend the entire long weekend trapped in this deserted-for-the-weekend, miles-from-anywhere suburb, than to suffer that smug, philosophically-superior look on The Statistician's face as he jump starts the Microbus. Even worse, if the persnickety VW refuses to co-operate, she might have to face the horror of spending three hours in a car with The Statistician and his whiny, high-maintenance, country-club wife.

She looks out through the kitchen window, over the identical squares of chemically fertilized golf-green lawn and the identical asphalt-paved driveways of the identical beige-stucco McMansions lined up in perfect geometric order.

Like, why did I ever move here? My parents were right. I don't belong in the suburbs, no matter how cheap the rent. I really need to get out of here.

Like, now.

She breathes in slowly, and then she calls The Statistician.

THE REBEL
ALLIANCE

*"She'll make point five past light speed. She may not
look like much, but she's got it where it counts, kid."*

— HAN SOLO, ABOUT HIS SPACESHIP *THE MILLENNIUM FALCON*,
TO LUKE SKYWALKER, FROM THE MOVIE *STAR WARS*, 1977

"**W**ow," says The Statistician as he peers into the blackened engine compartment of Hippie Avenger's inherited Microbus, "How many miles does this thing have on it? Five hundred thousand? A million?"

"I don't know," Hippie Avenger says. "The mile-counter thingy has flipped over so many times that …"

"The odometer, you mean."

"The mile-counter thingy, yeah."

"Wow," The Statistician says again. "I can't believe this old engine still runs."

Hippie Avenger glances at The Statistician and Time Bomb's shimmering black Cadillac Escalade SUV, and then at the sad-eyed cartoon animals on the PLEASE DON'T POLLUTE OUR WORLD sticker on the front fender of the old VW.

"Not all of us can afford to drive the Death Star," she says.

"Hey, a *Star Wars* reference!" The Statistician cheers. "Good for you!"

When he was a kid, *Star Wars* was The Statistician's favourite movie, despite its obvious scientific flaws, like Han Solo referring to a parsec as a unit of time rather than distance, or all of those fiery explosions in the oxygen-free void of space. He and The Drifter, with their officially licensed action figures and plastic spacecraft, used to stage epic sagas on the top bunk in their shared bedroom.

The Statistician fastens the jumper cable clamps onto the terminals of the VW's ancient battery, and says, "If our SUV is the Death Star, then your Microbus is an X-Wing fighter."

"I don't know what that means," Hippie Avenger admits. She suspects that she has just been insulted, but she isn't sure, since she's never seen *Star Wars*, despite being made to feel as if the space saga was somehow her own generation's Woodstock.

"The Empire," Statistician explains, "were the bad guys. They had the big, expensive, technologically advanced Death Star. The Rebel Alliance, on the other hand, flew rickety, outdated, patched-together old X-Wing fighters."

"And the people in the Rebel Alliance were, like, the good guys?"

"Indeed. Here on Earth, Luke Skywalker would be driving your Microbus into battle. And he would probably vote for the Green Party, too."

Hippie Avenger smiles. So he meant it as a compliment. With The Statistician, she is never sure.

He taps a knuckle on the faded "Reduce, Reuse, Recycle" sticker affixed to the front bumper of the Microbus between the "Impeach Nixon!" and "Free Leonard Peltier" decals.

"And," he continues, "in addition to being the good guys, the Rebels were being environmentally conscious by *reusing* old space fighters, instead of wasting precious raw materials building new ones."

Hippie Avenger's smile disappears. "Are you mocking me?"

"No! This is one of the few bumper stickers on your van that I agree with. The Earth has *finite* resources, so we can't go on digging and burning them up *infinitely*."

"Then why the friggin' *Battleship Escalade*?"

"It's hers, not mine." The Statistician says, gesturing toward the sleeping Time Bomb, whose face is pressed against the passenger window of the enormous SUV. "I usually just take the subway to the university, but she refuses to use public transit at all — too many 'allergens and toxins' in the air, apparently."

He raises the long, heavy hood on the Escalade and connects the jumper cables to its massive black battery.

"I thought she should get a nice, efficient little Honda Civic to run around the city in," he continues, "but apparently people who live in *our* neighbourhood don't drive *Hondas*. Apparently she feels '*empowered*'" — he makes quotation marks in the air with his fingers — "by driving something large enough to generate its own gravitational field. Personally, I blame the feminist movement."

"Hey! Buying a gas-guzzling tank has nothing to do with …"

"Aw, relax. I just said that to annoy you. Her mother bought it for her. She's got one, too, so they're both very *empowered*. Now, jump into your VW and we'll see if we can get you *empowered*, too."

Hippie Avenger climbs onto the frayed driver's seat of the Microbus and turns the key. After a few wheezy, laboured turnovers, the little engine sputters, coughs, and then begins running earnestly. Its irregular burbling is music to Hippie Avenger's ears; she won't be trapped in the suburbs for the weekend, nor will she have to endure the trip to the cottage in the Death Star with The Statistician and Time Bomb.

"Shit!" cries The Statistician from within the SUV's cavernous plastic and fake-wood interior. "Everything's gone dead! What the …?"

Time Bomb's eyelids flutter, and she mumbles sleepily, "Jump-starting another vehicle can trick the ATS into disabling the onboard computer so the engine won't run."

"ATS?"

"Anti-Theft System."

"You didn't think to tell me this until now?"

"You need a special electronic gizmo to reset it," Time Bomb says. "It'll be tough to find a mechanic who can do it, since it's the long weekend. I guess we'll just have to stay home." She pauses before adding, "Darn the luck."

Hippie Avenger wanders over beside the open driver's-side window of the Escalade. She offers tentatively, "Well, like, if you two want to ride with me …"

"In *that* thing?" Time Bomb gasps. "My God! Does it even have CCAPS?"

"See-see-what?"

"Climate Control and Air Purification System! *Air conditioning*, for God's sake! My hair will be a disaster in this humidity."

Hippie Avenger says, "The Microbus comes equipped with a top-of-the-line NAS. It's an older technology, but it always works."

"NAS?"

"Natural Airflow System."

Soon the old VW is rattling along a northbound highway, humid summer air blasting through its open windows. Hippie Avenger is behind the wheel, and The Statistician rides shotgun.

Time Bomb sneezes three times, *"Ah-shee! Ah-shee! Ah-SHAH!"*, then curls up in a fetal position on the rear bench seat. She grumbles something about "toxins and allergens" before falling into a drooling, snoring slumber.

*

They have been on the road for nearly an hour when The Statistician abruptly says, "'Meat is Murder!'", quoting the translucent sticker affixed to the windshield above the dashboard in front of him. "Actually, killing another human being is *murder*. Meat is *food*."

"*Vegetables* are food, too," says Hippie Avenger, knowing that she's chomping on the former high school Debating Champion's bait.

She remembers the time that The Statistician passionately advocated atheism to Teens Need Truth co-chairs

SuperKen and SuperBarbie, and then turned around and argued for the existence of God with the vociferously atheist Psycho Superstar. When everyone else proclaims to be liberal, The Statistician is conservative. When they are warriors, he's a pacifist. When they are socialists, he's a capitalist.

"Humans are *omnivores*!" he says, the volume of his voice rising. "We're designed to eat vegetables *and* meat. It's why we've got incisors in our mouths. It's why we come equipped with the enzymes and acids particular to our digestive system. It's why …"

It's the same argument they've been having since high school, and Hippie Avenger inevitably runs out of ammunition before The Statistician does. She's not in the mood to fight this battle yet again, so she says, "I didn't put that sticker there. My parents did."

"But you're a *vegetarian*, aren't you?"

He might as well have replaced the word *vegetarian* with *idiot*.

"Actually, I eat a bit of meat once in a while now."

"Oh," he says, deflating.

To The Statistician, a good debate is as essential to a road trip as the road itself. When they were kids, sitting in the back seat of their father's Buick Skylark en route to some horrible tourist destination like the World's Biggest Ball of Twine, he and The Drifter would wile the time away arguing about almost anything; whether Spider-Man was more or less than half as strong as Superman, would Mario Lemieux have scored as many goals as Wayne Gretzky if he hadn't been hampered by injuries and illnesses, would it be better to colonize the Moon or Mars, and so on.

"So you eat meat now, eh?" The Statistician says. "That's a sudden change in philosophy, indeed. What about all the cuddly, friendly animals?"

Hippie Avenger says, "I was becoming iron deficient."

"Anemic," says The Statistician.

"Yeah, iron deficient. Like, especially during my menstrual cycle. When all that blood gushes out of your body, you lose a lot of iron, and, like … or would you rather I didn't get into the details?"

"I'm married, remember? Believe me, I know all about the magic and mystery of the menstrual cycle."

They both glance back at Time Bomb, who is still snoring on the bench seat. Hippie Avenger wonders if Time Bomb is having her period right now, or if she's always so distant and irritable.

"So, how often do you go carnivore, then?" The Statistician wonders. "A few times per month? A three-to-one ratio of vegetarian to omnivorous meals?"

"Oh, just about every day," Hippie Avenger says, "but it's not like I order the twenty-four-ounce porterhouse or the triple cheeseburger. Only a few ounces at a time, and, like, not for every meal."

She is surprised when The Statistician says, "That's pretty sensible, really. Each meat-producing animal consumes way more than its weight in corn, soy, and other grain, which could just as easily be eaten directly by humans. North Americans in particular consume much more meat than they need to, which is *not* efficient use of food energy. It's simple mathematics, really. You don't expend five units of food energy to create one unit."

Well. This is hardly the adversarial debate she expected.

"I only buy free-range, grain-and-grass-fed meat," she says, with an intentionally haughty tone. "I will not buy factory-produced meat products, like, no matter what. Penning up animals, and force-feeding them chemicals and semi-edible waste until they're slaughtered is just wrong."

That ought to get him going, Hippie Avenger figures. But rather than trotting out the familiar counter-argument that

corporate agricultural methods are more economically efficient, or the rationalization that livestock are food, not per-
sonalities, The Statistician *agrees* with her.

"Indeed," he says. "Meat factories consume enormous
amounts of energy, pollute water supplies, and generate
ridiculous amounts of greenhouse gases. And all those antibiotics and hormones they pump into the animals get passed
onto the consumer. And, besides, the animals are much
better treated on free-range farms. There's no reason they
need to be *tortured* before becoming food."

"Like, when did you become so reasonable?"

"I've always been reasonable. Reason is my forte."

"So, you mean we, like, actually agree on something?"

"Indeed we do."

They ponder this for a while. As they travel farther from
the city, through farm country, the smell of tarmac and
exhaust fumes in the air is replaced by dust and manure,
and the road becomes bumpier and noisier.

"So what else do you want to talk about?" The Statistician says. "Good conversation makes a long trip seem
shorter."

"I don't know. What do you guys usually talk about?"

"Whenever we go anywhere, she takes an antihistamine,
two ibuprofens, a Gravol, and an Ativan, and she's asleep
before we leave the driveway." The Statistician shrugs. "Oh
well. At least she isn't complaining about anything when
she's unconscious."

"At least you've got somebody." Hippie Avenger says wist-
fully. "At least you're not travelling alone."

Even someone as literal at The Statistician knows that
Hippie Avenger is speaking metaphorically. He wants to
say something soothing, so this is what he comes up with:
"Well, as Oscar Wilde once said, '*Marriage is like a cage; one
sees the birds outside desperate to get in, and those inside equally
desperate to get out.*' Indeed, Oscar Wilde. Indeed."

Hippie Avenger sighs. "Actually, I think it was, like, the French philosopher Michel de Montaigne who came up with that one."

"*Indeed,*" comes the shrill voice of Time Bomb from behind them, "It, *like*, was de Montaigne."

The Statistician winces; his wife was only *pretending* to be asleep.

For the remainder of the trip, nobody says anything else.

THE PERFECT PAIR

*"When Captain America throws his mighty shield,
all those who choose to oppose his shield must yield!"*

— FROM THE THEME SONG FOR THE
TV SHOW *CAPTAIN AMERICA*, 1966

SUPERHERO PROFILE: SUPERKEN

A.K.A.: Sergeant Rock

SEX: Male **HEIGHT:** 6'3" **OWB (Optimum Body Weight):** 186.3 pounds **CBW (Current Body Weight):** 236 pounds

MILTARY ROLE: Officer Cadet (on medical leave)

SPECIAL POWERS: Former Honour Student, Star Athlete, Social and Moral Role Model.

SPECIAL EQUIPMENT: Titanium leg braces. Lots of cool Army-surplus field equipment.

SPECIAL VEHICLES: White Chrysler minivan (gasoline-fuelled internal-combustion-engine propelled); Invacare Rolls 900 Folding Wheelchair (SuperBarbie-propelled).

FAVOURED ELIXIR: Domestic beer.

SLOGANS/MANTRAS:
"If you don't stand behind our troops, try standing IN FRONT OF THEM!"
"Gay marriage is NOT MARRIAGE!", etc.

THE INDIFFERENCE LEAGUE

DID YOU KNOW?
SuperKen voted Republican in the last United States federal election, despite the fact that, technically, he does not have American citizenship. An investigation is pending.

Collector Card #10 — *Collect All 20!*

10/20

SUPERHERO PROFILE: SUPERBARBIE

SEX: Female **HEIGHT:** 5'10" **OWB (Optimum Body Weight):** 145.4 pounds **CBW (Current Body Weight):** 177 pounds

CIVILIAN ROLE: Former Team Captain, Olympic Candidate, University Scholarship Nominee

MILTARY ROLE: Officer Cadet's Wife.

SPECIAL POWER: The Power of Faith.

SPECIAL EQUIPMENT: Possibly bulletproof sports bra; The Bible; *Name Your Baby; Nine Months: What to Expect During Your Pregnancy;* FIRST RESPONSE Early Result Pregnancy Test Kit.

SPECIAL VEHICLES: White Chrysler minivan (passenger); Invacare Rolls 900 Folding Wheelchair (driver).

FAVOURED ELIXIR: Alcohol during pregnancy is a no-no.

SLOGANS/MANTRAS: "Family Values," "Pro-LIFE," "Jesus is my Co-Pilot," etc.

THE INDIFFERENCE LEAGUE

DID YOU KNOW?

Although SuperBarbie believes that lying is morally wrong, the knitted baby booties that she bought three years ago at Hippie Avenger's craft sale were not really a gift for her pregnant cousin Janey. The booties are still tucked away in her "Hope Chest," waiting to be worn.

Collector Card #11 — *Collect All 20!*   11/20

The Perfect Pair's arrival at The Hall of Indifference is announced by squealing brakes and crunching gravel. After missing the back corner of Mr. Nice Guy's grey Honda Civic by mere inches, their white Chrysler minivan comes to a rocking halt in a cloud of dust beside Hippie Avenger's VW Microbus. SuperKen is expressionless behind the wheel, while SuperBarbie occupies the passenger seat, smiling-yet-terrified.

Hippie Avenger, The Statistician, and Mr. Nice Guy, who have been unloading the luggage from the back hatch of the Microbus, freeze in position, stunned by the Perfect Pair's meteoric landing. The racket even momentarily wakes Time Bomb, who had complained of a migraine and excused herself to lie down inside one of the cottage bedrooms.

Swinging from side to side in the back window of the minivan is one of those diamond-shaped yellow signs that usually read BABY ON BOARD, but this one says VETERAN ON BOARD! Affixed below the window is a sticker shaped like a loop of ribbon, in green and brown camouflage colours, that reads I SUPPORT OUR TROOPS! A larger bumper sticker shouts, IF YOU DON'T STAND BEHIND OUR TROOPS, TRY STANDING IN FRONT OF THEM! There is a wedding-cake-shaped decal that proclaims, GAY MARRIAGE IS NOT MARRIAGE!, surrounded by several others, in red, white, and blue, that read: FAMILY VALUES," PRO-LIFE, and JESUS IS MY CO-PILOT.

"Wow," says The Statistician, "that was a close one. Jesus must be their co-pilot, indeed."

"Everyone is entitled to their own beliefs," says Mr. Nice Guy.

"Did I say that they weren't?"

Also on display on the back of the minivan is one of those chromed-plastic fish-shaped emblems with the word JESUS inside the fish's body. The Statistician points at it and says to Hippie Avenger, "I thought it was *Jonah* who was swallowed by the fish, not Jesus."

"Jonah was swallowed by a *whale*," says Hippie Avenger. "But if I remember correctly from my World Religions course, the fish was a symbol that early Christians used to, like, secretly identify themselves to other Christians."

"Perhaps it's not such a secret when you put the word *Jesus* in capital letters in the middle of the fish, hmm?" The Statistician muses.

"Don't be intolerant," Mr. Nice Guy says.

"I wasn't being *intolerant*!" The Statistician yelps, "I was just making an *observation*!" He reaches up to pull the rear hatch of the Microbus closed.

"Um, just leave it up for now," Hippie Avenger says. "Let it air out for a few minutes."

The real reason that Hippie Avenger is reluctant to close the back door of her parents' former shaggin' wagon is the collection of faded decals that they slapped on it so many years ago. As a professional soldier, SuperKen will probably not appreciate the slogans such as AN EYE FOR AN EYE MAKES THE WHOLE WORLD BLIND, or WHAT IF THEY HELD A WAR AND NOBODY SHOWED UP? As the ex-Co-Presidents of Teens Need Truth, both he and SuperBarbie will likely take issue with the sticker declaring that THE MORAL MAJORITY IS NEITHER, or the one that says A WOMAN'S BODY, A WOMAN'S CHOICE, or especially JESUS IS COMING — LOOK BUSY!

The Statistician, of course, pulls down the hatch on the Microbus anyway, making a point of studying the propaganda plastered on the rear ends of both the VW and the Chrysler vans. He declares, "Ooh! I feel a philosophical grudge match coming on!"

If SuperKen and SuperBarbie try to engage her in an argument, Hippie Avenger will fall back on her old excuse: "Hey, my parents put those stickers on, I didn't." This explanation may be wearing thin, though, since she's driven the Microbus for nearly ten years and she still hasn't made any effort to scrape off any of her parents' stuck-on beliefs.

"Be nice, okay?" says Mr. Nice Guy, mostly to The Statistician. "Let's leave politics, religion, and philosophy out here in the driveway."

"What's left to talk about inside, then?" The Statistician wonders.

SuperBarbie steps out though the passenger door of the minivan.

"Sorry about the dramatic entrance!" she chirps. "With his injuries, he probably shouldn't really be driving, but, y'know, he can just be so darned stubborn sometimes!"

"His injuries?" Mr. Nice Guy wonders.

SuperBarbie ignores the question and hands two books to Hippie Avenger, saying, "Hold these for a moment, would you please?" She scurries around to the other side of the Chrysler, followed by the sounds of the driver-side cargo door sliding open, grunting and sighing, scraping and clanging, and then more grunting and sighing.

Mr. Nice Guy calls out, "Um, anything I can help you guys with?"

SuperBarbie finally appears, pushing a wheelchair with SuperKen perched upon it like a King on Coronation Day. Both of SuperKen's legs are encased in robotic-looking titanium braces, and his knees and shins are crusted with scar tissue.

"Good Lord!" says Mr. Nice Guy. "What happened to you?"

"He's a War Hero!" SuperBarbie exclaims. "He was injured while serving in Afghanistan."

"Afghanistan?" says The Statistician. "I didn't know you were in Afghanistan." He turns to Hippie Avenger. "Did you know he was in Afghanistan?"

"Y'know," SuperBarbie says, "we *did* mention it in our annual Christmas newsletter."

This past December, The Statistician had continued his annual Yuletide tradition of carrying The Perfect Pair's star-and-cross-festooned summary of their personal successes and church-related activities directly from the mailbox to the recycling bin, while Hippie Avenger had stopped reading at their heartfelt appeal for signatures on their petition against sex education in schools. As such, both had missed the news about SuperKen's first actual combat duty since joining the military.

"I read it," Mr. Nice Guy proudly declares. "How long were you there before …"

"It happened right at the beginning of my tour of duty," SuperKen says.

"What happened?" The Statistician wonders. "Did you get shot?"

"Enemy anti-personnel initiatives were not a factor," SuperKen says, with what Psycho Superstar would have described as his "Sergeant Rock" voice.

"Bomb shrapnel? Grenade? Did you step on a land mine? What?"

"Neither Aerial Ordnance, nor Improvised Explosive Devices, nor Area Denial Munitions were factors in my injury."

"Well, Jesus, what the hell …?"

"Y'know, you could say 'gee whiz' instead," SuperBarbie interrupts.

"*Gee whiz*," The Statistician continues, "What the *heck* happened to you?"

"My division was flown in to secure the area after a pre-emptive strike on a suspected insurgent threat, and I was injured during the preliminary stages of the operation," SuperKen says. "However, I'm not at liberty to discuss any further details at this point in time."

"Indeed," says The Statistician.

"He's going to make a full recovery and rejoin the Good Fight soon," says SuperBarbie, panting as she struggles to push the wheelchair through the driveway gravel. That SuperKen has gained about fifty pounds does not make her job any easier.

"Here," says Mr. Nice Guy, "let me help you with …"

"No, no!" SuperBarbie insists. "It's a labour of love! He's my War Hero."

Hippie Avenger positions herself between the advancing Perfect Pair and the back of the Microbus, to prevent them from reading the quaint anti-war sentiments plastered all over it. Desperate for a distraction, she holds up the dog-eared hardcovered books that SuperBarbie had handed her, which are titled *Nine Months: What to Expect During Your Pregnancy*, and *Name Your Baby*.

"So," she says, "it looks like you two have, like, some *other* big news to share with us?"

SuperBarbie stops pushing the wheelchair and slumps over SuperKen's shoulder.

"No," she sighs, "unfortunately not."

Hippie Avenger's face glows red as she realizes that the round paunch hanging out over the waistband of SuperBarbie's lavender jogging pants is *not* being caused by a baby growing in there.

"Y'know, we tried and tried before he was sent to Afghanistan," SuperBarbie says. "Every day, sometimes more, but no luck."

"Well, *I* got lucky," SuperKen says.

SuperBarbie slaps him on the shoulder (not playfully) and snatches the two books from Hippie Avenger.

"Well, y'know, according to the reading I've done," SuperBarbie says, "positions that allow deep penetration and don't force the semen to work against gravity are best. Y'know, there's a reason the church advocates the missionary position!"

"Doggy-style is good, too," SuperKen adds helpfully.

"*We don't call it that!*" SuperBarbie barks. "But yes," she says, regaining her composure, "my honey is right. Both positions allow for the deep penetration and gravitational assistance required for of the sperm to reach the uterus. The missionary position increases the changes of conceiving a girl, and the, um, y'know, *hands and knees* position is what you do if you want to have a boy."

Although he has no idea why SuperBarbie is sharing this information with the rest of them, The Statistician nevertheless feels obligated to say, "I doubt there's any meaningful correlation between the gender of a couple's offspring and how they ..."

"I read it in here!" SuperBarbie says, brandishing her copy of *Nine Months: What to Expect During Your Pregnancy* (which was originally published in 1954). "Anyway, now with his legs injured, we can only use woman-on-top positions for intercourse, which don't really have the best chance for conception. So it's been a pretty rough road."

Finally, Hippie Avenger sees where SuperBarbie has been going with all this.

"Wow. How difficult," she says. "I'm sure it's been a trial for you both."

"Yeah," says Mr. Nice Guy. "How difficult."

"It's been a real uphill battle," SuperKen interjects, smirking.

"Indeed," adds The Statistician, who slides his fists in his pockets to conceal his half-mast erection. Although he finds her *rah-rah, y'know* personality rather annoying, the image of SuperBarbie bouncing up and down in the Ride 'Em

Cowgirl position is enough to activate his own underutilized baby-making tool.

"Well, y'know," SuperBarbie says, "if we just keep trying, maybe, God willing …"

"It's been fun trying!" SuperKen says.

"Stop it!" SuperBarbie cries, slapping SuperKen's shoulder again. "It's not about having fun!"

"Actually," Hippie Avenger says, "I was reading in a women's magazine the other day that the female orgasm actually creates a 'sucking' effect that can draw the sperm through the vagina and into the uterus faster."

"See?" SuperKen says. "It's not just a *duty*. Letting yourself enjoy it *helps*!"

A flustered SuperBarbie drops both books onto her husband's lap.

"Ow!" he cries, "Ow! Ow! My balls! Ow!"

"Oh, no!" SuperBarbie cries. "I didn't mean to! Oh, no! Are you okay, my honey? Are your testicles okay?"

While SuperBarbie prances around SuperKen, fretting that she has just inadvertently cluster-bombed his civilian sperm-manufacturing facilities, SuperKen winks at the others and points at the one war-themed decal on the Microbus that isn't at least partially concealed by Hippie Avenger's body.

"'Make Love, Not War,'" he says. "Yep, one is *definitely* more fun than the other."

SuperBarbie pounds SuperKen's back repeatedly with closed fists, then snatches the books from his lap. Clutching them to her chest, she elbows her way through the cluster of Not-So-Super Friends and scrambles up the wooden stairs into the cottage, crying "It's all for nothing! It's all for nothing!"

"Aw, honey!" SuperKen calls after her. "Come on, honey!"

She can be heard screaming, "It's all for *nothing*! *Nothing!*" until the door slams behind her.

SuperKen stands up, hobbles toward the cottage, and struggles up the cottage stairs after his wife.

"Hey!" Mr. Nice Guy yelps, "Don't you need your wheelchair?"

"No," SuperKen growls. "I don't need any fucking wheelchair!"

RIDDLE ME THIS ...

"*Since you'll be sticking around for a while, I'll leave you a riddle to work on: The more you take away, the larger it grows.*"

— THE RIDDLER, FROM THE TV SERIES *BATMAN*, 1966–1968

THE INDIFFERENCE LEAGUE

THE ORIGINAL EIGHT!!!
AND THEIR FAVOURITE
CHARACTER(S) FROM STAR WARS

THE STATISTICIAN
Han Solo/Princess Leia
(Wanted to be Han Solo,
wanted to do Princess Leia)

THE DRIFTER
Han Solo/Princess Leia
(The brothers think alike
on this topic)

SUPERKEN
Han Solo/Princess Leia
(See above)

SUPERBARBIE
Yoda
(At SuperKen's request,
though, she once dressed
up as Princess Leia for
Halloween)

HIPPIE AVENGER
No opinion
(Has not seen any of the
Star Wars movies)

MISS DEMEANOR
Han Solo/Princess Leia
(See above)

PSYCHO SUPERSTAR
No opinion
(Quote: "Star Wars is for fags!")

MR. NICE GUY
Luke Skywalker
(Still secretly wants to
become a Jedi)

Collector Card #12 — *Collect All 20!*

12/20

And once again Mr. Nice Guy and his friends are hanging out on the stony beach in front of his parents' cottage. They are gathered around a lakeside campfire, which crackles modestly under Mr. Nice Guy's care. He built the fire from pre-split hardwood purchased from a nearby farm, and he got it going with only kindling, matches, and wind from his own lungs; no gasoline, kerosene, Styrofoam or stolen wood. *It is an honest fire*, thinks Mr. Nice Guy. *A respectable fire. Yeah.*

It is a cool, overcast Saturday evening, exactly twelve years minus two days from the night they first named themselves The Indifference League. All of the stars are hidden tonight, but the light of the moon, diffused through a thin, low layer of cloud, coats everything with a silvery glow.

When one of the Not-So-Super Friends forgets and refers to one of the others by their actual name, Mr. Nice Guy reminds them of the pact they made over a decade ago. They've grown a bit tired of this charade, but they go along with it anyway. The Hall of Indifference is *his* cottage, after all, and the poor guy has had a tough year, with Sweetie Pie calling off their engagement and all that.

They are a smaller group this time around, just The Statistician, Hippie Avenger, Mr. Nice Guy, SuperKen, and SuperBarbie. The Drifter is still en route, Miss Demeanor emailed to say that she wouldn't be arriving until later, and of course Psycho Superstar is absent for obvious reasons.

Time Bomb, to the amazement of the rest of the League, actually made it through dinner without collapsing from a migraine or a fit of *"Ah-shee! Ah-shee! Ah-SHAH!"* sneezing. Mr. Nice Guy played it safe by eliminating the ground pepper from his "famous, trademarked" spaghetti, using only fried ground beef and canned tomato sauce with sugar and powdered garlic added in, none of which are on the long list of Time Bomb's "migraine triggers" or "dermatological and respiratory sensitivities." Nevertheless, Time Bomb spends exactly five minutes watching Mr. Nice Guy blow on the embers to get the fire going, then declares it to be "too fucking cold out here," and retreats to her bed in the cottage anyway.

The Statistician offers to accompany her inside to "warm her up," but the way she rolls her eyes tells him that he is in for yet another physical-intimacy-free evening. *Fifty-seven nights*, thinks The Statistician. *A new record.*

So, just five members of The Indifference League are present to enjoy the honest, respectable fire built by Mr. Nice Guy.

*

After pushing SuperKen in his wheelchair through the tall grass between the cottage and the beach, SuperBarbie wipes the sweat from her brow and plants their folding field marshal's chair as close as possible next to her War Hero. She used to sit on SuperKen's lap atop the ubiquitous army-surplus seat, but neither the chair's frayed, camouflage-green canvas nor SuperKen's damaged legs seem able to support the weight anymore.

Mr. Nice Guy and The Statistician have just unfolded their lawn chairs across the fire pit from The Perfect Pair, when Hippie Avenger arrives carrying a cooler full of beer and a couple of bottles of Chardonnay; she graduated from those puckeringly sweet vodka coolers around the time she started working at the art gallery, where complimentary wine is part of the sales pitch.

"Oops," she says, "I forgot to bring myself a chair."

"Take mine," The Statistician says, springing up and heading back for the cottage. "I'll go grab another."

Mr. Nice Guy pushes his chair closer to Hippie Avenger's right side, and says, "I would have gone to get a chair for you, you know."

"You're sweet," she says.

"I try to be," he says, admiring her behind as she leans forward to pour Chardonnay into the two red plastic cups she's set up on the lid of the cooler. As Hippie Avenger stretches to hand a cup to SuperBarbie, the top of her dress pulls tight against her left breast.

It's always bits and pieces with her, Mr. Nice Guy muses. *Glimpses and suggestions. Man, I would like to see what her whole body looks like underneath those potato-sack smocks she wears. Oh, yeah.*

"Hey," he says, "could I have some wine, too?"

"Oh, sure," Hippie Avenger says. She leans forward again, and Mr. Nice Guy holds his breath and watches. *Oh, yeah. Oh, yeah.*

"Taste it and tell me what you think," she says, handing him a sample of the wine. "It's what I serve to potential customers at the gallery."

Mr. Nice Guy makes a big show of swirling the wine around inside the plastic cup, sniffing it like he's drawing his final breath, and then swishing the wine around in his mouth, wearing an expression like he's trying to solve a complex equation.

It smells like cat piss and it tastes like rocket fuel, he thinks. *With a hint of lemon.*

"Sublime and delicious!" he declares. "Your taste is impeccable."

"Sublime and delicious!" SuperKen mocks him. "Did you turn impeccably *gay* since the last time we saw you?"

If Miss Demeanor were here, Mr. Nice Guy would definitely tear a strip off SuperKen for that insensitive remark, but since she's not, he decides to let it slide.

"Still a beer man," he grunts, "just wanted to try some wine." Then he bravely adds, "And a *real man* does what he wants. Without worrying what others think."

"Says the librarian to the warrior," SuperBarbie giggles.

"I'm not a *librarian*," Mr. Nice Guy protests. "I'm an *archivist*."

The Statistician returns and plunks his lawn chair down to the left of Hippie Avenger.

"Wench!" he cries, "A brown ale for this thirsty traveller!"

"Hey!" Mr. Nice Guy protests.

"He's just kidding," Hippie Avenger says. She reaches into the cooler and hands The Statistician a dripping brown bottle, then tosses a differently labelled brew to SuperKen.

"Light beer?" SuperKen protests. "*Queer* beer? Toss me real one, okay? Mr. Nice Guy can drink this one when he's finished with his *wine*."

Mr. Nice Guy decides to let it slide this time, also.

Hippie Avenger's second toss is more forceful than the first, and Tom Thomson High's former Male Athlete of the Year fails to catch it.

"Don't get up, sweetie!" SuperBarbie yelps. "I'll get it!"

She chases the bottle as it rolls clinking over the pebbles, and she soaks her sneakers when the surf tugs it into the water. When she finally hands the beer to her War Hero, he says, "Thanks, babe."

He's popped the cap and chugged down most of the bottle's contents before SuperBarbie has even settled back into the field marshal's chair.

"Don't get up, sweetie!" she says, jumping up again, and scrambling for the cooler. "I'll get you another."

"Thanks, babe," SuperKen says, grinning absently.

"He sure developed a taste for that stuff in the Forces," SuperBarbie says, almost apologetically.

After the beer-fetching routine has been repeated six times, SuperKen stands up from his wheelchair.

"Sweetie!" SuperBarbie says, "Please! Rest your poor legs. Y'know, whatever you need, I can do it for you!"

"I need to take a piss," he says. "You can't do *that* for me, honey. And, unlike Mr. Nice Guy, I don't do it sitting down."

Mr. Nice Guy doesn't say anything this time, either, but his fuse is getting shorter.

SuperKen sways from side to side as he hobbles away from the fire, disappearing into the moon-shadow behind a clump of tamarack that serves as the traditional outdoor urinal of the male Not-So-Super Friends.

"Would one of you guys go with him," SuperBarbie frets, "and make sure he's okay?"

The Statistician heads for the Pee Tree. "I've got to go anyway," he says.

"I would have gone with him, too," Mr. Nice Guy reassures SuperBarbie and Hippie Avenger.

"You're such a nice guy," Hippie Avenger says.

*

The Statistician positions himself in front of the Pee Tree beside SuperKen, and is about to unzip his own fly when SuperKen makes some alarming noises.

"Ohhhh! Uhhhhh!" SuperKen groans. "What are you … *uhhhhh! UhhhhhHHhh!"*

The Statistician glances down and sees that SuperKen is, with military precision and timing, stroking a stubby erection.

"Uhhhhh! OOHhhHHHHHMMmmm!" SuperKen snarls as he ejaculates onto a cluster of fragrant tamarack needles. When he's finally caught his breath, he whispers, *"Ahh, ahhmm* … listen … don't say anything about this to the wife, okay?"

"I understand," The Statistician says. "A man needs to take care of himself sometimes when nobody else is doing the job." Out of habit, he clears his throat and adds, "Indeed."

"Hey, man, I'm being taken care of well enough. Lately she's on top of me three times a day. It's friggin' *great*."

"Oh," says The Statistician. That *would* be great.

"She'll probably want to ride me again soon, so I need to empty the magazine of the love gun beforehand, if y'know what I mean."

The Statistician is forced to admit that he does not know what SuperKen means.

"Okay. Listen," SuperKen whispers. "It was bad enough that I had to wait until we were friggin' *married* to finally get into her. But, y'know, she's was so friggin' hot, I figured it would be worth the wait. And it *was*, my friend. Oh, my sweet Lord, it *was*. But she's got this whole you-can-only-have-sex-if-you're-trying-to-have-a-baby thing going on, right?"

"Um, I thought you had that you-can-only-have-sex-if-you're-trying-to-have-a-baby thing going on, too. You two *were* the co-presidents of Teens Need Truth."

"Do you remember the chicks in that group? Hotter than hell, every last one of 'em. As if Jesus was saying, *'Come on! Look at these babes! What are you waiting for? Sign up today!'* So I did, man, I did."

The Statistician marvels that SuperKen's impersonation of Jesus Christ sounds a lot like a used-car salesman on a late-night TV ad.

SuperKen continues, "But, sure, of course I want to have a kid. Children are the future! But I also want to have as much sex as possible beforehand. Because as soon as she gets pregnant, it's *over*."

He pauses to shake a drop of pearly seminal fluid from the tip of his diminutive unit.

"So, y'know, I've gotta purge the baby batter from the barrel of the bazooka as often as I can, 'cause when one of my men eventually breaks through the perimeter, I won't be firing the ol' SSM launcher again for a while."

The Statistician doesn't bother asking what "SSM" stands for.

SuperKen looks down as he zips up his pants.

"Ah, shit," he says, "I got some on one of my leg braces."

The Statistician reaches into the inside pocket of his tweed jacket and removes a handful of Kleenex, which he offers to SuperKen.

"Um, yeah, thanks," says SuperKen, "but I can't actually bend over to do it. Would you mind?"

With a furrowed brow and pursed lips, The Statistician obliges, tossing the Kleenex under the Pee Tree when the aluminum brace is clean.

SuperKen turns and limps back toward the fire. "Just between us guys, eh?" he says over his shoulder. "I don't want to hear another lecture about the sin of 'spilling my seed.'"

"Indeed," says The Statistician, who is finally able to release his own hose from the confines of his trousers to urinate.

The bazooka. The love gun. The SSM launcher. I've never had a nickname for mine.

Then something occurs to him.

Maybe my own wife is secretly also the you-can-only-have-sex-if-you're-trying-to-have-a-baby type. Maybe she would be more interested in having sex with me if she was trying to get pregnant.

I'll ask her tonight.

*

On the end of a straightened wire coat hanger, The Statistician is holding a bratwurst sausage in the flames. "Want it?" he asks Hippie Avenger.

She wrinkles her nose like she always does. "You mean, do I want to eat a tube full of chemicals and fatty, nutrition-free flesh cut from an animal that was cruelly imprisoned and force-fed hormones and antibiotics?"

"Just checking," The Statistician says.

"Why don't you leave her alone," Mr. Nice Guy says. "You know she's a vegetarian."

"I eat some meat now," Hippie Avenger says, shrugging.

"You do?" Mr. Nice Guy gasps.

"Yeah. Sometimes."

"She was anemic," The Statistician says. "Her body needed the iron. And the protein, too."

"Oh," says Mr. Nice Guy, visibly hurt. *He's* the one who listens to the women talk about their problems, *not* The Statistician.

"Listen," Hippie Avenger says to The Statistician, "if you cook up any sausages made from free-range chicken, I'll be first in line, okay?"

"I'll go into town and get some for you tomorrow," The Statistician says. "Nobody should have to go without sausage."

"Believe me," Hippie Avenger says. "I've gone, like, *way* too long without it."

"I know what you mean," mutters The Statistician, as he slides the bratwurst into the soft inside of a bakery bun lubricated with mustard.

Oh my God! Hippie Avenger thinks. "*I've gone way too long without it.*" *Like, was I being flirty with The Statistician?*

Then, an even crazier thought: "*Nobody should have to go without sausage.*" *Was he being flirty with me?*

She decides that this is impossible. *The Statistician? Flirty? Come on. He's all brain, no feelings. There's a reason they called him The Android.*

Still, her arousal response has a hair-trigger these days, and this maybe-but-probably-not flirtation is enough to stir that familiar warm, aching, tugging feeling inside her. *Nobody should go without sausage, indeed.* The Purple Pal will be seeing some action tonight.

"*I* can go into town and get some organic meat for you," Mr. Nice Guy says. "I know a little butcher shop out on one of the concession roads."

"Thanks," Hippie Avenger says, patting his shoulder. "That's sweet of you."

"So then," The Statistician says, waving the blackened bratwurst in its bun, "who wants to eat this tube full of chemicals, fat, hormones, and antibiotics?"

"I'll take it," says SuperKen, from his wheelchair. "They feed us worse stuff than that in the Forces."

"My hero," SuperBarbie says, fetching the sausage for him. "I'll bet you're hungry, poor thing. It's been a tiring day for you, with all that driving and everything. Maybe we should go get some sleep now."

SuperBarbie gives SuperKen a subtle look, the type of expression that The Statistician never gets from Time Bomb, but that he may have just received from Hippie Avenger. But probably not. It was likely just the shifting light from the fire deceiving his eyes, combined with his desperate libido playing tricks on his brain. It was probably nothing.

SuperKen munches on the bratwurst and winks at The Statistician as SuperBarbie wheels him around the fire and toward the cottage.

Mr. Nice Guy glances conspicuously at his Super G Digital Athletic Chronometer, which reads 11:11 p.m. He stretches, yawns, and says, "Well, it's late. I think I'll turn in, too." He turns to Hippie Avenger, who is wearing an expression similar to the one demonstrated by SuperBarbie, and he says, "Care to join me?"

"That's okay, dude. I think I'll stay out here for a while."

"Oh," he says. "Okay."

He slumps toward the cottage, sighing after every third step.

After Hippie Avenger hears the cottage door bang shut behind Mr. Nice Guy, she slides her lawn chair a bit closer to The Statistician's.

"So, you work with numbers, right? So, like, what's your favourite number?"

The Statistician laughs. "I don't have a favourite number," he says. "Numbers are numbers. One number isn't better than another. A number is only a word or symbol, or a combination of words or symbols, used in counting or in noting a total, or a particular symbol assigned to an object so as to designate its place in a series, or …"

"My favourite number is seven," she interrupts. "When I was a little kid and I was learning to draw my numbers, seven was my favourite. And it still is."

"Why? Why is seven better than, say, thirty-one, or sixty-one, or ninety-seven, or one-hundred-thirty-one, or …"

He continues naming every seventh prime number after seven until she interrupts him again.

"I was only a little kid. I only knew the numbers between one and ten. And just the primary and secondary colours, too. Red, yellow, blue. Orange, green, purple."

The Statistician almost says, "The correct scientific term is *violet*," but he stops himself.

"Purple is still my favourite colour. I coloured skies blue and grass green and the sun yellow like I was supposed to, but any time there was a choice, I coloured it purple. Flowers, cars, clothing, houses, all purple. I had boxes of crayons with barely used red and oranges, but the purples were all worn down to stubs. And seven was my favourite number to draw. My parents' refrigerator was covered in pages of purple sevens stuck up with random letter and number-shaped magnets."

She pauses.

"Do you want to know why I liked sevens so much?"

"Indeed." He really does want to know.

"Because seven was the number you could make the most choices about. You could draw it with clean, straight lines. You could draw it with a little arch in its back."

She unconsciously leans forward, pushes her chest out a little, shakes her hair behind her shoulders.

"You could put a little horizontal line through the middle, to give it some girth. Or you could put a serif on the bottom to anchor it to the ground. Or a little overhang on top, like a tin cottage roof. You had the freedom do any, or some, or none of these things."

She settles against the frayed back of the lawn chair.

"And no one would tell you that it wasn't right."

Hippie Avenger stares up into the sky. There is a slender break in the shell of cloud overhead, through which a few of the brighter stars shine.

"Pretty, eh?" The Statistician says. "Light from stars that might already be dead."

"Might they maybe still be alive?" she wonders.

"Possibly," he says. "Mathematically speaking, though, it's likely that …" he stops himself.

She says, "They're still alive to us, I guess."

"I guess," he agrees.

They both look up for a long time. Gradually, like fluff-edged theatre curtains, the clouds part until almost the whole glittering sky is revealed.

"Eight," The Statistician says.

"Hmm?"

"Eight," he repeats. "My favourite number is eight."

"I thought you didn't …"

"The infinity symbol is perfect for what it represents: a quantity without bound or end. It twists and turns in on itself forever. The set of real numbers is uncountably infinite," he says, as if he is reciting ancient scripture from parchment. "That single, simple mathematical truth still fascinates me."

He sighs.

Hippie Avenger actually heard The Statistician sigh.

"And," he says, "if you draw it in one fluid motion, rather than two circles on top of each other like they tried to make me do it in school, an eight is like an infinity symbol rotated vertically."

"Cool," she says.

"Plus," he adds, "when I was small they were fun to draw."

"When were you ever small?" She is about to say something else, but she stops herself.

"What?" The Statistician says. "What were you going to say?"

"Nothing. You'll think it's stupid. You'll say it's a meaningless coincidence."

"Try me."

"Well," she says, "my birthday is on the eighth of May." She shrugs.

"Mine is December twenty-first," he says. "Twenty-one is a multiple of seven." Then, almost reflexively, he adds, "Not that this fact is statistically meaningful." Then he turns his head to one side, and says, "But it is cool."

"You called something *cool*," she teases.

"Some things are."

The Statistician smiles. Hippie Avenger can hear his breathing. It is slow and deep.

They both just stare up into space for a while.

"Hey," Hippie Avenger says, "do you still get Friday afternoons off?"

"It's the main fringe benefit of being an untenured professor."

"I noticed that *Star Wars* is playing next week at the rep theatre up the street from the gallery."

"I thought you hated *Star Wars*," he says. "I thought that was the one thing you had in common with my wife."

"I don't hate *Star Wars*," Hippie Avenger says, "I just never got around to seeing it. But I think I'd like to see it now."

"It's a date, then," The Statistician says, who is slightly embarrassed that his voice cracked like that when he said it.

"Cool," says Hippie Avenger, whose eyes are rimmed with tears from the smoke from the fire.

FORTRESS OF SOLITUDE

"There are many questions to be asked. Here, in this Fortress of Solitude, we will try to find the answers together."

—Jor-El, Superman's father, from
the movie *Superman Returns*, 2006

All of the stars are hidden tonight, but the light of the moon, diffused through a thin, low layer of cloud, coats everything with a silvery glow, making the beam from the Norton Commando's headlamp almost unnecessary.

From her perch on the back of the motorcycle, The Stunner looks up into the sky. There is a slender break in the shell of cloud overhead, through which a few of the brighter stars shine, following them as they speed along this hard-topped back road.

"How much farther?" she calls out over the Norton's steady roar.

"We just passed the cottage," The Drifter calls back.

"We just passed the cottage?" she echoes. "Why?"

"The sky is clearing," he says, "And there's a place that I want you to see."

The bike leans as they turn from the road and onto a narrow, stony path. The Drifter downshifts, and the engine howls as the Norton carries them up the steep trail. Leaves and needles brush their shoulders as they climb. The Stunner tightens her hold around The Drifter, clenches the seat between her thighs to keep from sliding off the back of the bike.

The Drifter cuts the engine as they reach the top. The brakes squeal as the Norton comes to a halt on a narrow finger of stone that juts out between the black expanse of water below and the opening sky above.

They dismount and set their helmets on the ground beside the bike, which radiates heat from the long ride. The Stunner unties her hair and shakes it loose around her shoulders. The Drifter pulls a blanket from a saddlebag, spreads it across the smooth stone at the edge of the promontory.

They sit atop the ragged blanket, shoulder to shoulder, and they both look up for a long time. The pinging and crackling sounds from the cooling engine eventually subside, and the wind drops from a whistle to a whisper to silence. Gradually, like fluff-edged theatre curtains, the clouds part until almost the whole glittering sky is revealed.

"Wow," The Stunner finally says.

"I found this place once when I was out hiking by myself. I used to climb up here when I wanted to get away from everyone else," The Drifter says. "This was my Fortress of Solitude."

"Fortress of Solitude," The Stunner repeats. "I like that."

"Not my idea. It's the name of Superman's secret fortress in the Arctic, where all of the knowledge of Kryptonian civilization is stored in crystal form, and where …" he pauses. "Sorry. I was a bit of a comic-book geek when I was a kid."

"Geeks become heroes, I think," she says, running the tip of her index finger from The Drifter's rough, stubbled cheek to his chin, "with experience."

The Drifter mirrors the gesture, tracing the smooth skin of her face with a calloused fingertip. Then he reaches into the front pocket of his jeans, opens his palm to reveal what he has removed: two small, smooth stones. One is shaped like a boomerang, slate-grey, cut through with slight, white parallel lines. The other is pink, flecked with metallic specks, almost perfectly round, except for a slight bump on one side.

"I found these on a beach in France, among millions of other stones. The tide had pushed them together just like this."

The bump on the pink stone fits perfectly into the concave side of the slate-grey boomerang.

"They are from different places. They are made from different materials. And yet they are like two halves of a whole, like they were shaped and eroded and moved around by the forces of nature just so they could eventually fit together like this."

He spreads his fingers, and says, "Take one."

She hesitates.

"Which one?"

"Whichever one you want."

Her fingers hover over his open palm.

"Is this supposed to mean something?"

He shrugs.

"Only if you want it to."

She takes the pink stone from his open palm, closes her hand around it to preserve its warmth.

"Can we sleep out here tonight?"

"Won't you be cold?"

"You'll warm me," she says.

IN COSTUME

"The claws and the costume get 'em every time!"

— Catwoman, from *Catwoman #11*, 1994

The sky outside is still dark when Miss Demeanor arrives in her baby-blue Subaru Outback. She enters the cottage with a backpack slung over one shoulder, closes the door gently behind her, and tiptoes across the plywood floor.

"Hi," whispers a voice from the shadows.

When Miss Demeanor's eyes adjust to the darkness, she sees Mr. Nice Guy stretched out on one of the sofas.

He glances at his Super G Digital Athletic Chronometer. It is 4:11 a.m. He must have drifted off for a while.

"I waited up for you," he says.

"You didn't have to do that, buddy," she says.

"I wanted to."

In the dim moonlight filtered through the dusty curtains, Mr. Nice Guy can see that Miss Demeanor is wearing blood-red lipstick, and a figure-hugging black minidress, with long sleeves that cover her tattoos. Her hair is long, black, and needle-straight.

"Wow," Mr. Nice Guy says, "You look just the way you used to."

"Yeah, I grabbed the dress and the wig from the costume closet at the cabaret."

She was dressed something like this on the night of her one and only dalliance with Mr. Nice Guy, out there on the pebbles so many years ago.

Did she dress like this for me?

"I thought it might be easier this way," she says.

He feels his pulse throbbing throughout his entire body. *Oh yeah, oh yeah, oh yeah.*

"Hey, it's late," he says, trying to be cool, trying to put this exactly the right way. "All the bedrooms upstairs are full. Well, except for mine, that is. Maybe, um … maybe do you want to share my room tonight?"

"You mean, sleep in the …" Now she realizes what he's thinking, and says, "Oh, no. No, no, no, no, buddy. There isn't going to be any Ben-Affleck-in-*Chasing-Amy* scene for you tonight."

His *tabula rasa* face tells her that he didn't catch the reference. The Drifter would have recognized it right away.

"Look," she says, "I just decided to dress like my old self to make it a bit less shocking for the others. I want to wait until the time is right to tell them. I didn't mean for you to think that you … you know, that you and I … that we …"

"Right. Yeah," says Mr. Nice Guy. "Okay. Yeah. Of course. Yeah."

"Look," she says, "I'll just sneak into the Hipster's room for tonight, okay?"

"Oh. Okay. Yeah. Sure."

She hears the alarm is his voice.

"Don't worry, buddy," she laughs. "I won't try to get her to switch teams or anything. I'll sleep on the floor."

Mr. Nice Guy steps forward to hug her, but Miss Demeanor turns and heads directly for the stairs, with her backpack still slung over her shoulder.

"Keep your head up, sport," she says, "I think you might still have a shot with her."

SECRET IDENTITIES

"That's one trouble with dual identities, Robin. Dual responsibilities."

— BATMAN, FROM THE TV SERIES *BATMAN*, 1966–1968

THE INDIFFERENCE LEAGUE

ADVENTURE SCORECARD:
NUMBER of SEXUAL PARTNERS

Miss Demeanor: 96
(61 Female, 35 Male)

Psycho Superstar: 17
(Including 12 partners who
were paid by the hour)

SuperKen: 9
(Despite signing the same
contract as SuperBarbie)

Hippie Avenger: 6
(Four of the six were guys
she met at Phish concerts)

Mr. Nice Guy: 3
(Technically speaking, he
only got to "Second Base"
with Hippie Avenger, and
"Third Base" with Miss
Demeanor, but he counts
them anyway)

The Drifter: 4
(All post-motorcycle)

SuperBarbie: 1
(Due to the Pre-Marital
Virginity Contract she
signed in high school)

Time Bomb: 21
(4 were employees of Time
Bomb's father. 3 were employees of Time Bomb herself)

The Stunner: 26
(The number is reduced
to 4 if fellatio-only encounters are excluded)

The Statistician: 2
(The number is reduced
to 1 if fellatio-only encounters are excluded)

13/20

T he Statistician wakes up and smells the coffee. Literally. He rubs his eyes and glances at his watch on the bedside table. 6:11 a.m. It is unlikely that any of the other Not-So-Super Friends are awake this early on a Sunday morning. Who could possibly be brewing coffee already? Maybe Mr. Nice Guy has one of those coffee makers with a timer on it.

Regardless, The Statistician's foggy brain sure could use some caffeine. He didn't get much sleep last night, with The Perfect Pair banging their headboard against the wall in the adjacent room, over and over and over again, making at least four separate attempts to start a baby growing inside SuperBarbie. He was also pretty sure he also heard soft moans of pleasure emanating from Hippie Avenger's room down the hall.

These nocturnal noises did nothing to put Time Bomb in the mood for similar exertions. Neither did his whispering in her ear, "Hey, sweetie, do you want to have a baby?"

She responded by snorting, "After all the work I've put into getting my abs in shape? Yeah, right!"

And thus they set a new record for marital abstinence: fifty-seven consecutive nights.

The Statistician rolls out from under the covers, staggers through the door, and pauses in the hallway at the top of the open staircase. The dark aroma of the coffee wafts up from the kitchen, and triggers a vague memory in his waking brain: it smells like the inside of The Protégée's apartment. He remembers the warm, slick feel of her lips around him, and his erection surges against his biplane-patterned pajama pants.

He can't go downstairs in this state, so The Statistician tiptoes back into the wood-panelled bedroom, and he holds his breath to avoid waking Time Bomb. When he has finally saturated the Kleenex plucked from the box on the dresser, he allows himself to exhale, slowly, quietly. The Kleenex lands with a wet slap inside the metal trashcan beside the bed.

Time Bomb stirs, but does not wake.

The Statistician rebuttons the fly of his pajama pants and tiptoes down the creaky cottage stairs. Coffee time.

When he is halfway down, he sees her standing at the kitchen counter, pouring the black liquid from an aluminum carafe into an assortment of mugs. His feet fly out from under him, and there is a racket like an off-tempo Saturday-morning-cartoon drum roll — b*umpBUMP-bumpBUMP bangBANGkaTHUMP!* — as The Statistician descends the rest of the staircase on his ass.

She spins away from the counter, rushes toward him, stops halfway. The aluminum carafe slips from her grip, clattering on the floor. Coffee splatters everywhere.

The Statistician is sprawled on the tile floor at the bottom of the steps, heart pounding, adrenalized. He sees her stoplight-yellow panties under her short black skirt. *Proceed with Caution. Prepare to Stop.*

"What are *you* doing here?" she says to him.

"What are *you* doing here?" he says to her.

"Hey, bro," The Drifter says as he wanders into the kitchen. "You okay?"

"Uhhhhhhh," says The Statistician.

The Drifter helps his older brother to his feet.

"Your eyes are as big as saucers. I hope you haven't got a concussion."

"Ummmm, just a little dazed by the fall."

"Hey, I see you've met my girlfriend. Her Not-So-Super Friend nickname is 'The Stunner.' I picked it for her."

"The Stunner," The Statistician repeats. It takes a moment for his sleep-deprived, impact-addled brain to put it together: *My brother's new girlfriend is The Stunner. The Stunner is The Protégée. The Protégée is my brother's new girlfriend.*

"Uhhhhhhh," he says again, rubbing his temples.

"He'll be okay in a moment, I think," The Drifter says to The Stunner. "When we're all here together at this cottage, we call my brother here The Statistician,"

"Umm, hello, Statistician," says The Stunner, her eyes as wide and dark as The Statistician's.

"Um, yes," The Statistician says, "hello, um, Stunner."

Their fingers barely touch as they shake hands. They avoid looking directly at each other, as if they might turn into pillars of salt.

"Hey," The Drifter says cheerfully, sliding his arm around The Stunner's slender waist. "I fell for her the first time I saw her, too."

"Ha," The Statistician laughs weakly, rubbing the bruises darkening on his behind and lower back.

"Ha, ha," laughs The Stunner, who is just as shocked to see her former statistics professor here as he is to see her.

*

The noise of The Statistician falling down the stairs wakes everyone else in The Hall of Indifference, and soon the other Not-So-Super Friends wander downstairs, yawning, stumbling, not-so-ready-for-action.

First comes Mr. Nice Guy, who wipes up the spilled coffee with a handful of Charmin Extra-Absorbent Paper Towels. He is followed a few minutes later by Time Bomb, who, despite sleeping for most of the previous day, is nevertheless sluggish and raccoon-eyed. Hippie Avenger skips down the stairs, radiating Peace and Love. Her extended, multi-orgasmic self-pleasuring session resulted in a very satisfying night's sleep.

"Hey!" cheers Hippie Avenger, "look who else is here!"

Miss Demeanor descends the stairs, wearing the same clingy black outfit as a few hours earlier, her glistening she-vampire lipstick reapplied.

"God," Time Bomb moans, "how do you manage to look so fucking hot first thing in the morning?"

"Never leave your bedroom without putting on your lipstick and your nylons," Miss Demeanor says, sitting next to Time Bomb at the square, rough-hewn dining room table.

"I could put on a ball gown and have my makeup, hair, nails, and brows professionally done," Time Bomb says, "and I still look like shit if I wake up before noon."

"Hey, I wouldn't kick you out of bed," Miss Demeanor says, catching a look from Mr. Nice Guy that says, *Already?* She adds, "I mean, if I were a guy."

The Perfect Pair are last to join the group at the kitchen table. They are "morning people," and, to use one of Super-Barbie's own expressions, they are even more "bright-eyed and bushy-tailed" than usual. After twenty minutes of listening to the legs of their bed hopping percussively on the floor directly over their heads, each of the other Not-So-Super Friends quietly wonder if The Perfect Pair has finally achieved their objective of getting one of SuperKen's sperm into one of SuperBarbie's eggs. Since she always has "that glow," it's difficult to know for sure if the mission was successful. Either way, SuperKen looks happy. He's limping more than usual.

The Stunner is instantly liked by everyone when she brews up another pot of her sacred coffee blend for the drowsy group of anti-heroes. When she's poured a second cup for everyone, she heads for the back door and says, "Well, since all the bedrooms are taken, I think I'll go outside and start pitching our tent."

Damn, thinks Mr. Nice Guy, watching her recede from the room, *she's making* me *pitch a tent.* Then, as if there is a comedy-club audience in his head, he adds, *In my PANTS!*

"I'll go give her a hand," The Statistician says.

"Hey, that's nice of you, bro," The Drifter says. "I think you'll like her. She's really something, eh?"

"She certainly is."

The Statistician closes the door behind him as he steps outside.

*

Mr. Nice Guy wanders over beside The Drifter, who sips his coffee in front of the dining-room window, watching The Stunner untie the rolled-up tent from the luggage rack over the rear fender of the Norton Commando. The Statistician stands off to one side, arms folded.

"Looks like your brother and your girlfriend are having quite an animated discussion," Mr. Nice Guy observes.

"Cool," says The Drifter. "They're really hitting it off, eh? I really want him to like her."

"How could he not like her?" Mr. Nice Guy muses, as he watches The Stunner on her hands and knees, smoothing weathered red canvas across a patch of flat, grassy ground.

My God, what a body, thinks Mr. Nice Guy. *Oh, yeah, stretch like that! Oh yeah, oh yeah, oh yeah. Nice! Nice! Nice!*

"Sorry?" says The Drifter. "Did you say something?"

"Oh, I said, 'nice!' Like, wow, that is one nice bike you've got there. Yeah."

"Are you crazy?" Hippie Avenger says, partly to Mr. Nice Guy and partly to The Drifter. "There's nothing *nice* about it."

Mr. Nice Guy shrugs. "Hey, I was just being …"

"I know it looks a bit beaten up," The Drifter says, "but it's really quite reliable."

"Why on earth did you have to go and get yourself one of those *things*?" Hippie Avenger scolds The Drifter. "Like, what's with this male obsession with speed, anyway?"

"It's not about the speed," The Drifter says. "It's just about being … exposed, I guess. To the open air. To the surroundings."

"It's dangerous," says SuperBarbie, in a matriarchal way.

"*Life* is dangerous," The Drifter says, shrugging.

"We just don't want you to die," adds Hippie Avenger, her eyes glassy.

"But someday I *am* going to die, whether you guys want me to or not."

"You don't have to go *looking* for it," Hippie Avenger says.

"Should I just wait around for it to find me instead?" The Drifter says, his sandpaper voice becoming even more gritty than usual. "Should I sit at a nice safe desk in some generic office cubicle, or in front of a nice safe TV in some cardboard-box suburb, and wait around for a heart attack or a stroke to come take me away?"

The bit about the cardboard-box suburb strikes a chord in Hippie Avenger. She shifts in her seat, sucks on the lip of her coffee cup.

"Why should I settle for that?" The Drifter continues, his raspy voice calm and even. "I'd rather risk dying on my bike, while seeing things I've never seen, going places nobody else ever goes, feeling the wind on my face and the vibration of the engine through my body, than to wait trembling and alone inside a box for death to come get me."

The Drifter pauses. He isn't accustomed to being listened to by everyone in the room. Not in this crowd, anyway.

Hippie Avenger lays the trump card. "We've already lost one friend to a motorcycle crash. I can't take another phone call in the middle of the night, telling me that someone I care about has …"

Then she winces, looking tentatively at Miss Demeanor. She didn't mean to mention Psycho Superstar. Not yet, anyway. Nobody has had enough to drink.

"Well," The Drifter says, "with all due respect to Jake, he had a motorcycle for an entirely different reason than I do. He was only in it for the speed, for the quick-fix adrenaline rush." He looks at Miss Demeanor and adds, "No offence."

"None taken," she says. She knows that Psycho Superstar was into *her* for the same reason.

"But that's not what I want out of it," The Drifter continues, his voice like a tradesman's rough hands across smooth, soft skin. "I'm in it for the slow, satisfying journey, with lots of stops along the way. I want to take in the scenery and breathe in the air. I'm not interested in the short, fast thrill ride. I want that long, scenic, magical trip, with lots of twists and turns and hills and valleys. I don't want just the simple thrill of motion; I want that feeling of time and space wrapping around me, making me whole."

Everyone in the room equipped with a clitoris understands exactly what The Drifter means. And it's not just what he said. It's also the way he said it.

SuperKen sees SuperBarbie's doe-eyed expression, and he rolls his eyes and whispers to Mr. Nice Guy, "What's with the freakin' Jack Nicholson impression, eh?"

"Yeah!" Mr. Nice Guy sniggers.

"It's not an affectation," The Drifter says, "if that's what you guys mean. I got pretty badly dehydrated a couple of times in South East Asia. More than once I breathed toxic air, and a couple of times I mistakenly drank things that never should have passed though my throat. It all changed my voice. And it changed me, too."

Neither SuperKen nor Mr. Nice Guy say anything else. They are unaccustomed to The Drifter talking back like this.

"Tell us more about your trip," SuperBarbie says.

"It must have been amazing," says Hippie Avenger.

The Drifter has changed. He's grown. He's no longer just The Statistician's little brother. He's something else now. And they want to know more.

*

Just outside the window, the conversation is animated.

"But, but," The Statistician stammers, "I thought something had *happened* between us."

"It was just a blowjob," says the girl for whom fellatio is but one step from a handshake on the intimacy scale, to the man for whom the Quest for a Blowjob has been the Holy Grail of his adult life.

"As far as the university is concerned, there's nothing preventing us from being together now," The Statistician says, pacing back and forth in front of the half-assembled tent. "I've submitted the final grades!"

He gave her final theoretical paper a mark of 100 percent without even looking at it. He knew the calculations were perfect, because he'd done them himself.

"There *is* something preventing us from being together now," The Stunner says, continuing to knock tent pegs into the ground, avoiding The Statistician's eyes. "I'm seeing somebody now."

"Seeing *somebody?* You're *seeing* my little brother, for crying out loud! You're seeing my *little brother*."

"How was I supposed to know he was your brother? We met in a Chinese noodle place. And he's really not so little."

The Statistician continues pacing back and forth, rubbing his temples.

"But I thought …"

"It was just a blowjob."

"But …"

"It was just a blowjob."

The Statistician stops pacing.

"It was more than that to me."

"Please," The Stunner says. "I'm sorry, okay? Don't make it into more than it was. It was nothing."

"Well, then," he says, "I suppose you won't mind if I tell my brother about it, then. I'm sure he'll agree that it was *nothing*."

"Please don't tell him."

"Well, if it really was *nothing*, I don't see why ..."

"Please don't tell him!"

"Why shouldn't I?"

"If you care about him, you won't tell him."

"If I care about him, I *should* tell him."

"Please don't."

"Why not?"

"Because ... because I think I might be falling in love with him."

"You *think* you *might* be *falling* in love with him. There are a lot of variables in that sentence."

"I think I'm in love with him."

"You *think* you're in love with him."

"I'm in love with him."

"You're *in love* with him."

"I love him."

"You *love* him? Oh, come on! You just met!"

"I love him."

"You love him."

"Yes." The Stunner kneels in the flattened grass beside the tent. "I love him."

The Statistician straightens to his full height, feeling the pain in his back and buttocks from his tumble down the stairs.

"Well, then," he says, "I guess that makes everything all right, doesn't it?"

The Stunner wipes the tears away, and says, "Okay. Listen. You don't tell your brother, and I won't tell your wife. Deal?"

The Statistician's breath catches in his throat. He hadn't even *considered* including Time Bomb in his calculations. How could he have forgotten to include that variable?

"And that, my Protégée," he says, turning toward the cottage, "is an equation that balances."

ALTER EGOS

"The Blue Raja is my name. And yes, I know I don't wear much blue and I speak in a British accent, but if you know your history it really does make perfect sense."

— THE BLUE RAJA, FROM THE MOVIE *MYSTERY MEN*, 1999

ADVENTURE SCORECARD: (Part One)
PERSONALITY/TEMPERAMENT TYPES

The Statistician
**Myers-Briggs Personality Type: Introvert/
Intuition/Thinking/Judging**
Keirsey Temperament Type: Rational Mastermind
Examples: Isaac Newton, Stephen Hawking

Although The Statistician had often been heard to calling
psychology a "pseudo-science," he nevertheless agreed
completely with the assessment of his personality, and
that people of his type likely do make up less than 1
percent of the population.

The Drifter
**Myers-Briggs Personality Type: Introvert/
Intuitive/Feeling/Perceiving**
Keirsey Temperament Type: Idealist Healer
Examples: William Shakespeare, Albert Schweitzer

The Drifter didn't pay much attention to the test results.
His body was leaving for overseas later that month, and
his mind was already over there.

14/20

ADVENTURE SCORECARD: (Part Two)
PERSONALITY/TEMPERAMENT TYPES

SuperKen
Myers-Briggs Personality Type: Extrovert/ Sensing/Feeling/Judging
Keirsey Temperament Type: Guardian Provider
Examples: JC Penney, William Howard Taft

SuperKen was Super Pissed Off that SuperBarbie tested as "thinking" and a "supervisor," while he, The Man, was judged to be "feeling" and a "provider."
His judgment: "This test is bullshit!"

Mr. Nice Guy
Myers-Briggs Personality Type: Introvert/ Sensing/Feeling/Judging
Keirsey Temperament Type: Guardian Protector
Examples: Jimmy Stewart, Mother Teresa

It wasn't that SuperKen cried out "WIMP!" when Guardian Protectors were described as being well-suited for social work, child care, and nursing; what really bothered Mr. Nice Guy was that he shared three out of four Myers-Briggs categories with SuperKen.

Collector Card #15 — *Collect All 20!*   15/20

Breakfast has been served by Mr. Nice Guy, and all the current members of The Indifference League are seated around the dish-littered dining-room table, sipping coffee, poking forks at stray chunks of scrambled egg.

SuperBarbie is flipping through her dog-eared copy of *Name Your Baby.*

"Y'know," she says, "It's interesting how often the meaning of a person's name reflects their true nature."

"Gee," says Miss Demeanor, from across the table, "what does *your* name mean, Gilda Jane? Something good, I'll bet."

"Hey, Miss Demeanor," Mr. Nice Guy says, in a mock-scolding tone, "This is The Hall of Indifference! We use our superhero names when we're here."

"Sorry, buddy," says Miss Demeanor, resisting the strong urge to roll her eyes back into their sockets.

The Statistician, The Drifter, and Hippie Avenger glance at Miss Demeanor with eyebrows subtly raised in sympathy, then at each other, their eyes communicating the same message: *For how much longer are we going to go along with this?*

"Well," says SuperBarbie, missing the loaded-glance exchange, "according to the book, my first name means 'Covered in Gold,' and my middle name means 'God is Gracious.' Imagine that. Which reminds me … we all forgot to give thanks before we started eating."

She nudges SuperKen, who is parked beside her in his wheelchair, shovelling a third helping of ketchup-slathered eggs into his maw.

"Good food, good meat, good God, let's eat!" SuperKen mumbles as he chews. "That ought to cover it."

"Very funny," SuperBarbie says to him in a stage whisper. "You can pray for forgiveness in church today." Then she says to Mr. Nice Guy, "Does that cute little chapel up the road have a late-morning service?"

SuperKen mouths the words *no no no* at Mr. Nice Guy, who says, "Every Sunday at nine and eleven!"

That will fix him for those "queer beer" comments from last night.

SuperBarbie claps her hands. "Then we've got plenty of time to make the second sermon!"

"Come on!" SuperKen protests, "We're on vacation! The Lord will understand if we take one weekend off!"

"Faith is a full-time duty," SuperBarbie says. She flips open *Name Your Baby* again, and evangelizes to all gathered around the table, "Do you know what this book says about my husband? It says that his first name means 'lofty or exalted.' It says that his middle name means 'strong and manly.'"

She pats SuperKen on the shoulder. He will be going to church this morning whether he wants to or not.

"Does anyone else want to know the meaning of their given names?"

The other Not-So-Super Friends continue slurping and chewing.

"Well, let's start with the newest member of our little congregation, then," SuperBarbie says to The Stunner, "It says here that your name means 'Helper of Men' or 'Disbelieved by Men.'"

The Stunner is seated at the opposite corner of the table from The Statistician, as mathematically distant from him as she can be. The Statistician sends a dubious glance across the hypotenuse, which she tries to ignore.

"I know the story," The Stunner says. "My dad was really into Ancient History. It was the name of a Trojan princess. Her prophesies all turned out to be true, yet they were ignored by the men in power."

Mr. Nice Guy and SuperKen share a similar thought: *Nobody is ignoring you now, baby.*

The Drifter smiles at The Stunner and says, "'The Helper of Men.' I like that." Then he says to SuperBarbie, "Don't bother looking up my name. It won't be in there. As the second-born, I got saddled with Mom's maiden name."

"*Maiden* name," SuperKen taunts. "*That* explains a few things."

"Good one!" Mr. Nice Guy laughs. *Better him than me.*

"Was it the army that made you so homophobic?" The Drifter asks SuperKen. "Or did something else happen?"

"Homophobic? Afraid of *faggots*?" SuperKen retorts. "It'll be a cold day in hell when I'm scared of *fairies*."

"Nice," Miss Demeanor says, straightening her spine and pulling her shoulders back, like she used to do just before engaging Psycho Superstar in one of their infamous screaming matches. "What if one of your friends was secretly gay? How would you feel then?"

Mr. Nice Guy braces himself. *Is she going to tell everyone now? At breakfast?*

"I'm pretty sure at least *one* of these guys is gay," SuperKen chortles.

The Drifter runs his hand down The Stunner's back, and says, "You've met my girlfriend, right?"

Mr. Nice Guy adds, "I'm not gay, either, okay?" He notices Miss Demeanor clamp her teeth onto her blood-red bottom lip, so he adds, "Not that there's anything wrong with being gay. Although I'm not."

"Maybe we should ask your ex-fiancée," SuperKen says.

"She must have called it off for *some* reason."

Everyone stops slurping coffee. Silverware ceases to clink. Mr. Nice Guy looks down at his white tube socks. Everyone else glares at SuperKen.

SuperBarbie is desperate to break the vacuum her husband has created, so she says breezily to The Drifter, "Well, hey, if your *first* name isn't in here, then what about your *middle* one?"

"I haven't got one," says The Drifter.

"Our parents believed that one name per child was sufficient," The Statistician says.

"Let's look up yours, then!" SuperBarbie squeals. She flips through *Name Your Baby*. "Here it is! Your name means 'spearman.' How interesting."

"It means almost the same as *swordsman*," SuperKen sniggers.

"Indeed," says The Statistician. He avoids making eye contact with either Time Bomb or The Stunner.

As SuperBarbie flips the pages, Hippie Avenger says, "Like, don't bother looking up mine, okay?"

"Oh, I've already found it," SuperBarbie says. "It says that your name is a derivative of 'Karl,' which is itself a derivative of 'Charles'. How very interesting. I suppose the feminine form of 'Charles' would be …"

"It's a mistake," Hippie Avenger says, shaking her head. "My name is a mistake. My parents meant to name me 'Karma,' but someone misspelled it on the application for my birth certificate."

SuperKen sniggers some more. *"Karma?"*

"Yeah, yeah, I know," Hippie Avenger sighs. "It's a flower child name. I didn't get to choose it. Or my parents."

"At least they didn't name you *Sunshine*," SuperKen says. "Or *Rainbow*."

"They were both on the short list,' "Hippie Avenger admits.

"What about your middle name?" SuperBarbie suggests.

"Aw, it doesn't matter."

"Come on," SuperBarbie coaxes, "this is supposed to be fun."

Hippie Avenger blushes. "Look, it's just another dumb hippie name."

"I can't believe I've known you for all these years, and I don't know what your middle name is," The Statistician says. "Tell me."

He catches a cold look from Time Bomb.

"Tell *us*," he revises.

"Grace," Hippie Avenger says. "My middle name is Grace."

She waits for SuperKen to mock her. He doesn't.

"You don't have to look it up. It means what it means. I know it doesn't suit me."

The Statistician says, "I think it does."

Time Bomb huffs and rolls her eyes.

"As much as *anyone's* name suits them," he hastily adds.

SuperBarbie turns to Miss Demeanor. "It says here that *your* given name is actually the feminine form of the male name Raymond."

"Wow, Hipster," Miss Demeanor says, her back arching, her eyes narrowing to slits, "you and me both have names that were originally *guys'* names. I guess that makes Super-Barbie here a lot more feminine than either of us, eh?"

"Hey, I wasn't implying anything like that!" SuperBarbie says.

"You're usually implying *something*," Miss Demeanor says. She uncrosses and crosses her legs. As always, her short, tight skirt gives all the men a reason to look, but none of them do, for fear of getting caught.

SuperBarbie clears her throat emphatically and continues. "Anyway, your first name means 'Mighty Protector.' And your middle name means 'Warrior Maid.'"

"How about that," says Miss Demeanor. "Not bad. I was expecting something like 'Godless Harlot,' or 'Faithless Slut.'"

"I … you … I didn't …" SuperBarbie stammers. "Y'know, I apologized a long time ago about that."

"I remember," Miss Demeanor says, clenching her fists. "Your apology was, *y'know*, *so* sincere."

"Um, what does *my* name mean?" Mr. Nice Guy sputters, hoping to create a distraction.

This reminds him of the time when Miss Demeanor was working on her undergrad degree in psychology, and she had everyone complete Myers-Briggs Personality and Kiersey Temperament tests. Almost *nobody* was happy with their results. It was *so* tense. That was *supposed to fun*, too.

"What does *my* name mean?" Mr. Nice Guy repeats.

SuperBarbie flips to the front of the book, and says, "Oh. Right. Uh … 'Dweller at the Thicket.' Whatever that means."

Mr. Nice Guy has a vivid, high-definition memory of when Miss Demeanor was still furry down there. He feels the tickle on his lips and nose. That bittersweet scent fills his nostrils.

"More coffee, anyone?" he yelps. "I'll make more!"

He scurries into the kitchen with the carafe held at crotch level.

"And, last but not least," SuperBarbie says, aiming the cover of *Name Your Baby* at Time Bomb, "your first name means 'Wealthy One,' and your middle name means 'Sorrow.' Well. I wonder what …"

"You know what?" Time Bomb erupts, throwing her cutlery down and leaping up from the table, "Fuck you, you patronizing cow!"

Name Your Baby drops to the floor. SuperBarbie's jaw drops almost as far.

"I know you think I'm just some high-maintenance rich-bitch," Time Bomb says, "but have the guts to say it to my face! You don't have to make shit up about my name!"

"But … I … but …" SuperBarbie stutters, reaching for the fallen book, "I was only reading what it says in here."

"You know what else?" Time Bomb hisses, glaring at everyone seated at the table, "I know you all call me 'Time Bomb,' too, okay? Insulting me behind my back is bad enough, but you don't have to do it right in front of me! Fuck all of you!"

Time Bomb storms out of the cottage, slamming the storm door so hard behind her that the glass cracks.

"Happy now, *'Covered in Gold'*?" Miss Demeanor says. "Pleased with yourself, *'God is Gracious'*?"

"But it says so right here!" SuperBarbie protests, frantically flipping pages. "Her name means 'wealthy one,' after Shylock's daughter in *The Merchant of Venice*. And her middle name means 'sorrow,' from the Spanish term for the seven sorrowful occasions in the life of St. Mary, Santa Maria de los …"

"Well, if that's what the *book* says," Miss Demeanor says, "then I guess that makes it all okay. The *book* justifies anything you do or say, doesn't it?"

Then she turns on The Statistician.

"Are you going to just sit there, or are you going to go comfort your wife?"

The Statistician looks confused. Eruptions like this are everyday occurrences in their household. Trying to reason with her just makes it worse. She storms off, and eventually she returns, sedated.

"Fine, then," says Miss Demeanor, "I'll go myself."

She leaves the cottage to go find Time Bomb.

There is no sound, other than the burble of coffee brewing in the kitchen. There is no motion, other than the dust particles slowly drifting through the sunbeam that cuts through the window.

"Fortress of Solitude?" The Drifter says to The Stunner.

"Definitely," she says.

They jump up, grab their helmets, pull on their riding boots, and a few minutes later they roar away on the Norton Commando.

SuperKen winks at SuperBarbie. "Hey, babe … would you like to go for a ride with *me*?"

"It's time for church, now," SuperBarbie snaps. She stands up and wheels her husband away from the table. SuperKen still has his fork in his hand.

Only The Statistician and Hippie Avenger remain at the table when Mr. Nice Guy wanders in from the kitchen with the refilled carafe. "More coffee?" he offers.

Hippie Avenger says, "Maybe tomorrow you should serve decaf."

SUPER HEROINES

"We've always been ready for female superheroes. Because women want to be them and men want to do them."

— FAMKE JANSSEN, ABOUT PLAYING JEAN GREY
IN THE MOVIE *X-MEN*, 2000

ADVENTURE SCORECARD: (Part Three)
PERSONALITY/TEMPERAMENT TYPES

SuperBarbie
Myers-Briggs Personality Type: Extrovert/
Sensing/Thinking/Judging
Keirsey Temperament Type: Guardian Supervisor
Examples: George Washington, Judge Judy

SuperBarbie was pleased that she and SuperKen were the same in three of four categories, which she interpreted to mean that they were destined to marry. And SuperBarbie LOVES Judge Judy!

Miss Demeanor
Myers-Briggs Personality Type: Extrovert/
Intuitive/Feeling/Perceiving
Keirsey Temperament Type: Idealist Champion
Examples: Charles Dickens, Martin Luther King, Jr.

"Damn right I'm an Idealist Champion."
Nobody argued with her.

ADVENTURE SCORECARD: (Part Four)
PERSONALITY/TEMPERAMENT TYPES

Time Bomb
Myers-Briggs Personality Type: Introvert/ Sensing/Thinking/Judging
Keirsey Temperament Type: Guardian Inspector
Examples: Queen Victoria, Queen Elizabeth II

Although Time Bomb's answer to most of the questions on the test was "Who cares?," she nevertheless enjoyed being in the same category as two British queens.

Hippie Avenger
Myers-Briggs Personality Type: Introvert/ Sensing/Feeling/Perceiving
Keirsey Temperament Type: Artisan Composer
Examples: Bob Dylan, Mozart

Hippie Avenger noted that her parents would love the Bob Dylan parallel.
She also noted that she and The Statistician were complete opposites in three categories. She thought, *Well, that disproves the "opposites attract" theory, doesn't it?*

Both Hippie Avenger and The Statistician offer to help Mr. Nice Guy wash the breakfast dishes, but he insists, "No, no, no, I'll take care of it! You guys just go have some fun!"

So now they are lounging in the living room, waiting for everyone else to return to The Hall of Indifference: SuperKen and SuperBarbie from church, The Drifter and The Stunner from their motorcycle ride, and Time Bomb and Miss Demeanor from wherever they are.

The Statistician is perched awkwardly at one end of the musty, bowed cottage sofa. The lumpy cushions are uncomfortable against his bruised back and butt. Hippie Avenger is lying on the couch beside him, her head on the opposite armrest, her knees up, her toes dug in under his right leg. She's reading a copy of *Harrowsmith* magazine.

The Statistician is trying to read the title article in the *National Geographic* called "What Darwin Didn't Know," but Hippie Avenger's long cotton dress has fallen back onto her thighs, and he's distracted by her lean calf muscles, her perfect round kneecaps, her *café au lait*–coloured skin.

Terrific legs, The Statistician muses, *absolutely terrific. Top ten percentile.*

She pushes her toes in farther between The Statistician and the plaid sofa cushion.

"Mmmmm," she says. "You're warm."

The hem of her dress slides further down, revealing the sort of smooth, tapered thighs that The Statistician adores.

Revision, he thinks. *Top* five *percentile. And she shaves them, too; that's a pleasant surprise. How has it taken me so long to notice? It's those damn smocks she wears. Like hanging cheap motel drapes over a Monet.*

Time Bomb and Miss Demeanor storm up the stairs of the deck facing the lake, and then they burst into the living room through the sliding glass door.

"We're *baaaaaack*!" Miss Demeanor cheers.

"Hey!" Time Bomb shouts, "What are you guys up to?"

Hippie Avenger tugs her toes out from under The Statistician's thigh, bolts upright on the sofa, and smoothes her dress down over her legs.

Why did I do that? She wonders. *We weren't doing anything wrong. We were just reading.*

Time Bomb's hair hangs in wet strands. Miss Demeanor's eye shadow blackens the trickles that drip from her lashes. Their dripping clothes cling to their bodies. Their skins are speckled with goosebumps, their nipples painfully erect.

Mr. Nice Guy hears the commotion and emerges from the kitchen.

"We found an inflatable raft on the beach," Time Bomb says, suppressing giggles.

"Oh, that raft has a leak," Mr. Nice Guy says.

"No shit," says Miss Demeanor. "We kinda found that out the hard way. In the middle of the freakin' lake. Good thing we can both swim."

"Sorry," says Mr. Nice Guy. "I was going to patch it today."

"Well, get it patched, then, mister," Miss Demeanor cheers, "'cause me and Time Bomb are going back out!"

The Statistician looks quizzically at his wife.

"I don't care anymore," says Time Bomb. "Call me Time Bomb. I don't give a shit."

She grabs Miss Demeanor's hand. "Let's go get our bathing suits on!"

"I didn't bring a bathing suit."

"I brought four."

And nine pairs of shoes, The Statistician muses. *To a cottage.*

"You can wear my one-piece," Time Bomb suggests. "We're about the same size and shape."

"What you mean is, we're both totally sexy hotties! Let's go, girlfriend!"

They scramble up the stairs together, laughing maniacally.

"Have they been drinking already?" Mr. Nice Guy wonders.

"My lovely wife usually gets into the champagne just after breakfast," The Statistician says.

"And you remember that song Miss Demeanor used to sing," adds Hippie Avenger, *"'Happy hay, happy hay, smoke it any time of day!'"*

After much squealing from upstairs, Time Bomb and Miss Demeanor reappear.

Time Bomb descends the stairs first, wearing the impossibly slight two-piece that she bought while on vacation with her mother in the Bahamas. The Statistician had joked that it cost her over a hundred dollars per square inch, and he'd laughed at the prominently displayed brand name: "Wicked Weasel." According to Time Bomb, the brand was "all the rage." The Statistician suspected that she just wanted to be able to tell her Spa Buddy that she owned one, too; he never thought he would actually see her *wear* it. Nevertheless, here it is: the banana-yellow bikini top covers her nipples and not much else, and the thong-style bottom hides nothing of her Stairmaster-toned behind, and barely covers her professionally manicured pubic patch in the front.

"I hope you put on sunscreen," The Statistician says. "You know how sensitive your skin is to sunlight. And some of it has, um, never been exposed before."

"Oh, I slathered half a bottle of SPF-90 onto her body," Miss Demeanor says as she steps into the room. "I don't think a blowtorch could burn her now."

As usual, Miss Demeanor manages to shock everyone, even more than the nearly-naked Time Bomb has. It is strange enough to see the Goth-styled Miss Demeanor crammed into a flamingo-pink one-piece with a caricature of Miss Piggy across the abdomen, but that isn't what surprises her friends. Nor is it the nipple-piercings that are visible through the stretchy pink material. It's the tattoos.

The only body art Miss Demeanor used to display was the tiny Chinese symbol on her wrist, which Psycho Superstar bought her as a high-school graduation present. Now, her arms, shoulders, and back are covered with Chinese and pagan symbols, as well as detailed depictions of Bettie Page, Marilyn Monroe, Betty Boop, and other curvaceous icons from a bygone era.

Mr. Nice Guy's mouth hangs open just like The Statistician's, but not because of Miss Demeanor's tattoo display; he saw them earlier at the Cross/Fire Cabaret. Rather, Mr. Nice Guy is mesmerized by the sight of Time Bomb's nearly naked butt. He almost faints when she bends forward and says, "Miss Demeanor thinks a tattoo of Wilma Flintstone would look cute on my right cheek. She thinks I look like Wilma Flintstone. What do you think, honey?"

The Statistician's eyes bulge. "A tattoo? Seriously?"

"See?" Time Bomb laughs. "I told you he'd react like that."

"It's *your* body, not his," Miss Demeanor says, raising an eyebrow in The Statistician's direction. "Do what *you* want to do with it."

"But your ass is perfect the way it is!" The Statistician protests. "Why wreck it with a tattoo? Why not spray-paint graffiti on a Raphael? Why not build a roller coaster around the Taj Mahal?"

Miss Demeanor crosses her arms tightly, flexes her biceps and triceps, and squints at The Statistician.

"Oh, but they look good on *you*, though," he says.

"Rodney Dangerfield in *Caddyshack*," Miss Demeanor says. "Maybe you should get a tattoo of Rodney on *your* ass, buddy."

"Oh, right!" Time Bomb laughs. "Other than his wedding ring, he won't even wear *jewellery*. He doesn't even wear *cologne*."

In a squeaky voice, Miss Demeanor says, "We're going to pause here and we'll be right back with Gonzo, the Geek Who Fell to Earth. Miss Piggy. *Muppets from Space*."

"Oh my God!" Time Bomb says. "You're a pop-culture encyclopedia."

"And I look fucking hot in pink, too. Who knew?"

Mr. Nice Guy is unable to unlock his stare from Time Bomb's nearly naked buttocks as she and Miss Demeanor sway together like runway models through the sliding-glass door,

"Well," he says, "I guess I'd better go patch that leaky raft for them."

"You're a truly selfless man," says Hippie Avenger.

From where he's standing beside the sofa, Mr. Nice Guy can see most of Hippie Avenger's right breast though the neck opening of her smock. This gives him a fantastic idea!

"Hey, Hipster," he says, "why don't you throw on your bathing suit, too. There's room in the raft for four."

"I don't have a bathing suit," she says.

"Borrow one of Time Bomb's, then."

"Like, I'm not sure that's my style, dude."

"Just go in your underwear, then." *Oh yeah, oh yeah, oh yeah!*

"Um, I can't swim, buddy. Remember?"

Mr. Nice Guy had forgotten about that. "Oh. Right. Just a thought." *Oh, well, two out of three ain't bad*. He bounds through the living room and down the outdoor stairs, to catch up with Time Bomb's ass and Miss Demeanor's pierced nipples.

Hippie Avenger stretches out on the sofa again, kicks her legs free from beneath her long dress, and then submerges her frigid toes beneath The Statistician's warm legs.

"I could never wear either of those bathing suits, anyway," she says. "I just don't have the body for it."

"Sure you do," The Statistician says. "You've got terrific legs. You should show them off more." *Did I really just say that out loud?*

"Really?" she says.

"Really. They're mathematically perfect. Top five percentile." *What's wrong with me? I should have just stopped at "Really." The Geek Who Fell to Earth, indeed.*

"You think so?" she says. "Still, I'm just not like those two. I'm a pretty Plain Jane sort of girl."

"Well," The Statistician says, "Some of us would rather discover a beautiful gift inside a plain paper bag than a useless trinket wrapped in sparkles and ribbons."

Hippie Avenger leans forward and sniffs The Statistician's neck.

"So," she asks him, "you don't wear cologne?"

"No. I'm not inclined to slather corrosive chemicals on my skin just to smell like a pine tree. Or a saddle."

"Then how come you smell so good?"

"Just clean, I guess."

She sniffs again. He feels the cool tip of her nose on the back of his neck.

"Mmmmmm," she says. "Just clean."

Then she leans back and opens her *Harrowsmith* magazine again, wiggling her hips a little so the hem of her dress slides almost to her panties. *I guess my legs are kind of nice,* she thinks.

The Statistician resumes reading the *National Geographic*, inhaling deeply, noticing his own clean scent for the first time.

Both of their skins are speckled with goosebumps, too.

17

VERSUS

*"Don't make me angry.
You wouldn't like me when I'm angry."*

— David Banner (just before turning into The Incredible
Hulk), from the TV series *The Incredible Hulk*, 1978

When The Perfect Pair arrives back at The Hall of Indifference from their trip to the local church, SuperBarbie unfolds SuperKen's wheelchair, and he settles into it like a favourite La-Z-Boy recliner. She parks him on the opposite side of the coffee table in the living room of the cottage, where Hippie Avenger and The Statistician are reading their magazines.

"You guys are back early," Hippie Avenger says.

"Nobody told us it was an *interdenominational* service," SuperBarbie huffs.

"That must have been kinda cool," Hippie Avenger says. "Like, I should have gone with you."

"They mixed a bunch of Islamic, Hindu, and Buddhist crap into the real service," SuperKen gripes. "We got up and walked out. Well, *she* walked out. I *wheeled* out."

"The last thing my baby needs after being injured by *them* is to have to sit through a bunch of their chanting and screeching," SuperBarbie says. "It was just *offensive*."

The Statistician thinks to himself, *Did every single member of the Muslim, Hindu, and Buddhist religions beat up on SuperKen's legs? It's amazing that he can still walk.* He knows better than to say this out loud.

"I'm sure nobody meant to offend you," Hippie Avenger says. "A lot of different people take their vacations around here. They're probably just trying to be inclusive."

"*'Inclusive,'*" SuperKen repeats, rolling his eyes. "Our

society is too damned *inclusive*, if you ask me."

"Language, sweetie," SuperBarbie says.

"Sorry," SuperKen says, "but it makes me mad. We bend over backwards for all these freakin' minorities. And half of them are our *enemies*. If they don't like speaking English and worshipping Christ, they can all go the hell back home. It drives me nuts."

"Did you know that there is less than a *1 percent* difference in the DNA of any two human beings, regardless of their race?" The Statistician offers.

For the sake of his argument, he withholds the fact that the genetic difference between any human being and any *chimpanzee* is also less than 1 percent. He is desperate for a debate.

"When you look at it that way," The Statistician continues, "being biased against anyone because of their race is kind of asinine."

"Hey!" SuperKen says, "Did you just call me ...?"

The Statistician revises: "Such a bias would be *mathematically* asinine."

"Whatever," says SuperKen. "I still shouldn't have to listen to our *enemies* wailing in church with their freakin' diapers on their heads. This is a *Christian* country."

"It's a Christian *world*," SuperBarbie adds. "Christianity is the most popular religion on Earth."

"Is that true?" Hippie Avenger asks The Statistician. "Like, I would have thought that Hinduism or Buddhism would be number one, given the huge populations in Asia."

"Counts and estimates vary," The Statistician says, "depending on who is doing the counting and estimating. But it is generally held as true that Christianity is the most frequently observed religion, with approximately 2.1 billion practitioners, or about one third of the World's population. Next comes Islam, at about one-and-a-half billion, or 21 percent. At about nine hundred million, Hindus make up about 15 percent, and, rounding up, there are about three hundred and eighty million Buddhists. That's about 6 percent."

Hippie Avenger listens to the numbers roll off The Statistician's tongue like poetry.

"This is where the numbers get tricky, though. About another 6 to 12 percent of the population practises various indigenous religions, but it depends on the parameters used to define 'indigenous religion.' The number is higher if Chinese folk religions are included, lower if they've been mistakenly rolled into the figures for Buddhism. Anyway, about a third of 1 percent would be Sikh, and about a quarter of 1 percent would be Jewish. Confucians, Bahá'ís, Jainists, Shintoists, Scientologists, and pagans would account for …"

"So we win!" SuperKen cheers, raising his fists in the air like he's just scored a goal. "Christianity is number one!"

"But," The Statistician says, "Atheists, agnostics, and secular humanists blur the truth in the numbers somewhat, as they are often not included in official counts, nor do they have any formal way of declaring themselves on census forms and other surveys. So the figures I've …"

"Atheists and agnostics *do* blur the truth," SuperBarbie says. "Non-believers don't count in Heaven, so they don't count here, either."

"But that still leaves about four-and-a-half-billion people on Earth who aren't Christian. And I suspect that they *do* count here."

"Your *numbers* and your *science* can't explain everything," SuperBarbie says, pulling a frayed ottoman over beside SuperKen's wheelchair. She points at The Statistician's *National Geographic* magazine. "'*What Darwin Didn't Know*,'" she quotes from the cover in an I-told-you-so tone of voice. "*Hmmph.* It's about time somebody finally exposed the Theory of Evolution as a farce. And all you scientific types were willing to sell your souls for *that* lie."

"Well, actually," The Statistician says, "the article is about how Darwin couldn't have known anything at the time about the science of genetics, which is proving his Theory of Evolution to be *correct*. As subspecies intermingle and migrate, dominant genes are gradually eliminating certain recessive genes, causing species as a whole to …"

"The Theory of Evolution is *not* correct," SuperBarbie interrupts authoritatively. "We did not *evolve*; we were *created*. Evolution is a flimsy excuse for the miracle of life, invented by non-believers to promote non-belief. *Creation* is proof of God."

"For the sake of debate," The Statistician says, gearing up for a round of his favourite sport, "explain to me how you think the Theory of Evolution necessarily *disproves* the existence of God."

"The Darwinists say that all current living things came from previous kinds of living things," SuperBarbie says, pronouncing *Darwinists* the way she would say *Satanists*, and taking The Statistician's bait. She rises to her feet. "But The Bible says, 'And God made the beast of the earth after his kind, and cattle after their kind, and every thing that creepeth upon the earth after his kind: and God saw that it was good.'"

"Wow," The Statistician says, "You really know The Bible. Impressive. But, still, the question remains: could God not have *created* life to evolve? Did you know that when a man and woman of different races have a child together, their partner's dominant genes will cancel out the recessive genes of their own race, which usually carry most of the defects? And we're all intermingling all the time, so evolution is actually *improving* the human race. It's an amazing system, isn't it?"

SuperKen rolls his eyes and huffs, "It's amazing that anyone falls for that crap. It makes us soft on our enemies."

SuperBarbie quotes, "And God said, Let us make man in

our image, after our likeness … So God created man in his own image, male and female he created them.'"

"Okay, fine," says The Statistician, "but our debate isn't about *whether* the Earth was created or not. It's about whether Creation necessarily *excludes* the Theory of Evolution."

"It does," SuperBarbie says.

"It does," SuperKen agrees, hoping he'll get another ride out of it.

SuperBarbie folds her arms to signal that the debate has ended. For The Statistician, though, it has just begun.

"But the Earth itself slowly transforms itself constantly, right?" he persists. "Volcanoes erupt, mountains slowly weather away. The earth itself is in a constant state of flux. So why not the life upon it? Could God not have *designed* life to evolve, to adapt, to grow, to change, to *improve* with time?"

"'And God saw every thing that he had made, and, behold, it was very good.' God made the world perfectly the first time. It doesn't need to be *changed*."

"But can't some changes also be *good*?" Hippie Avenger interjects. "We all grow throughout our lives, become more mature, more understanding, more aware of what we want and need. I think Humanity has grown and changed throughout its lifetime, too."

"'He saw that it was good,'" SuperBarbie insists. "God did it right the first time. That's 'What Darwin Didn't Know.'"

The Statistician, realizing that there will be no sport in this argument, decides to retreat. "You should read the article," he says. "Then we can have a genuine debate about it later."

"I don't need to read an article in a *magazine*," Super-Barbie says, still standing. "I've read *The Bible*."

"If it helps at all," Hippie Avenger says, "I remember reading about something called The Eve Project. They isolated this single gene from a two-hundred-thousand-year-old female they found. Then they found the same gene in living women all over the world, from different countries and cultural backgrounds. It showed that all human beings, of all races and cultures, probably evolved from the same ancestral mother."

"Where did you find *that* bunk?" SuperBarbie scoffs. "In some supermarket tabloid?"

"In a university textbook, actually."

SuperKen guffaws. "No offense, but what *you* read in university hardly counts. You've got a diploma in Basket Weaving and Lunch!"

"I have a combined honours degree in Visual Arts and Women's Studies."

"*Women's Studies,*" SuperKen says, rolling his eyes back as far as they'll go. "Your degree might as well be printed on toilet paper. *Women's Studies.*"

"Look, I don't appreciate you implying that my degree is any less ..."

"Did anyone notice that their precious *Eve* Project didn't include *Adam*?" SuperKen rants. "Or that the study only sampled *women* from all over the world? That's Femi-Nazi *'research'* for you. Exclude men! Make men obsolete! Eliminate men!"

"The gene they sampled is only passed through mothers," Hippie Avenger explains, "so it would have been pointless for the researchers to include men in their ..."

"Bullshit," SuperKen says, waving his hand in Hippie Avenger's face, turning to The Statistician. "*They* invent the terms to put *us* at a disadvantage. Notice that the Femi-Nazis have invented a word for men hating women — *'misogyny'* — but there's no word for *women* hating *men*?"

"Actually," The Statistician says, "there *is* a word for that. *Misandry* is a hatred of men by women. Just like *misogamy* is a hatred of marriage, and ..."

"Well," SuperKen huffs, "I guess *you* should know all about *that* one, eh?"

The Statistician clears his throat and continues. "And a *misanthrope* is a hater of people in general. Get it?" At the moment, The Statistician is feeling slightly misanthropic himself.

"Whatever!" SuperKen says, squaring off against Hippie Avenger again. "So, what were your *Women's Studies* courses called, eh? Man-Hating 101? Introduction to Lesbianism? Advanced Studies in Whining and Bitching?"

Hippie Avenger jumps to her feet, steps over the coffee table, and stands before SuperKen's wheelchair. "What were *your* courses called? Killing Innocent Women and Babies 101? Introduction to Thwarting Societies Whose Cultures are Different from Your Own? Advanced Military-Industrial Profiteering?"

SuperBarbie grabs Hippie Avenger's shoulders and spins her around. "And I suppose *you* could do a better job protecting freedom and democracy from tyranny and evil?"

"So," Hippie Avenger says, cocking her head to one side, "you're okay with your own gender being mocked and maligned, but if anybody criticizes the military…?"

SuperBarbie pokes Hippie Avenger in the chest.

"*He* was injured fighting the good fight," she spits, "protecting *us* and the ideals that we stand for. While *he* was overseas, getting his legs smashed up, *you* were over here, sipping wine and selling *art*."

She pokes Hippie Avenger again.

"*He's* a War Hero. What kind of hero are *you*, sweetie?"

Another poke.

"Ow!" Hippie Avenger yelps. "Stop that!"

"If you don't stand behind our military," SuperBarbie says, "try standing in front of them."

"Yeah, yeah," Hippie Avenger says. "I read that one on the back of your minivan."

"Well, y'know," SuperBarbie says, the pitch and volume of her voice rising. "I read a lot of *baloney* on the back of your van! You should be ashamed of yourself."

She pokes Hippie Avenger in the chest again.

The Statistician expects Hippie Avenger to fall back on her usual excuse, *"My parents put those stickers on, I didn't,"* but instead she retorts:

"Oh, yeah? And *what* exactly, in your sacred opinion, should I be ashamed of?"

"'What if they held a war and nobody showed up?'" Super-Barbie says in a nasal voice, quoting one of the stickers on Hippie Avenger's Volkswagen. "What a bunch of bleeding-heart *baloney!*"

"'One Race — the HUMAN Race!'" SuperKen adds. "If we were all as naive as you and your pinko tree-hugger parents, there would be nothing left of our society."

Hippie Avenger snaps at SuperKen, "Leave my parents out of this, Captain America."

"Don't you *dare* talk to my husband that way," Super-Barbie fumes, "all of you ponytail-wearing, lefty liberals would be speaking *Arabic* if it weren't for men like him protecting your Godless, granola-munching asses!

"How am I *Godless?*" Hippie Avenger yelps. "I'm *Godless* because I prefer peace to war? The Bible calls Jesus the Prince of *Peace!* Is Jesus therefore *Godless?*"

"Don't you *dare* blaspheme!" SuperBarbie says, squinting, teeth bared. "*'Thou shalt not take the name of the Lord in vain'*! Have you heard that one before?"

She pokes Hippie Avenger again.

"As a matter of fact, I have," Hippie Avenger retorts. "It's the second commandment if you're Catholic or Lutheran, the third if you're Protestant or Jewish. And stop poking me."

"Then you've also heard *'Thou shalt not commit adultery'* right? And *'Thou shalt not covet thy neighbour's wife'*? I suppose it applies to our neighbour's husbands as well." Super-Barbie grins smugly.

"I don't like what you're implying," The Statistician says.

"We're just hanging out," Hippie Avenger adds.

"Just hanging out. Hmm. So I suppose you also know the commandment that says, *'Remember the Sabbath, and keep it Holy.'* But you chose to *hang out* all morning rather than observing the Sabbath, didn't you?"

"*'Thou shalt not kill.'*" Hippie Avenger says, glaring at SuperBarbie, then at SuperKen, then at SuperBarbie again. "Someone ought to remember that one the next time they launch a bunch of missiles at a village full of '*enemy*' civilians, eh? Or how about, *'Thou shalt not covet thy neighbour's house, or anything that is thy neighbour's'*? Someone should recite that one the next time a bunch of kids are sent overseas to die for another country's oil."

"Our enemies are getting what they've got coming to them," SuperBarbie hisses, poking Hippie Avenger again, *"An eye for an eye'!"*

"*'Makes the whole world blind,'*" Hippie Avenger says, quoting one of the stickers on her Microbus. "And stop fucking poking me!"

"Don't you swear at *me*, you bleeding lefty liberal!"

She pokes Hippie Avenger again.

Hippie Avenger grabs SuperBarbie's finger.

"Stop. Poking. Me."

"Let go of my finger."

"Don't poke me again."

"Or *what*?"

SuperBarbie pulls.

Hippie Avenger doesn't let go.

SuperBarbie pulls harder, digging her heels into the rug, flexing her muscular legs.

Hippie Avenger releases her grip.

SuperBarbie stumbles backward, landing on her ass on the ottoman behind her. She leaps right back up, lunges at Hippie Avenger, fists raised.

"Don't mess with me, you, you ..." Her face is flushed.

She's shaking. "I was the Female Athlete of the Year. What were you? You were *nothing*."

In his wheelchair, SuperKen hisses, "Yesss!" pumping his fist in the air, bouncing up and down on the seat of his wheelchair. His wife is *sooooooo* sexy when she's like this. It's like watching her spike a volleyball off an opponent's forehead. It's like that enraged predator face she used to make as her chest broke through the ribbon at the end of a race.

"Okay, okay," The Statistician says, pushing himself between SuperBarbie and Hippie Avenger. "This was only meant to be an academic conversation between four presumably rational and intelligent people. There is no need to get emotional. There is no need to get personal."

"That's why they called him The Android in high school," SuperKen says.

"See?" The Statistician says, "that's getting personal." He is feeling *quite* misanthropic now. "Why don't we all just agree to disagree, okay?"

SuperKen rises from his wheelchair and faces The Statistician. "So you don't have anything else to say on the subject, Mr. Know-It-All?"

"Let's just drop it for now," The Statistician says. "Before someone says something they'll regret later."

"So you're finished?"

"Yes. I'm finished."

"You lose, then," SuperKen says, folding his arms across his chest. "We win."

"Excuse me?"

"You lose. We win."

"But, terms of empirical evidence, we haven't even …"

"You retreated. You surrendered," SuperKen says. "So you lose. And we win."

"Are you kidding me?"

"Never declare war on a warrior, buddy," he says, slapping SuperBarbie's behind.

SuperBarbie winks at her husband, saying, "'And God said unto them, Be fruitful, and multiply, and replenish the earth.' C'mon, baby. Let's go upstairs."

She prances up the steps, invigorated. SuperKen unbuckles his belt as he hobbles up behind her.

Hippie Avenger and The Statistician collapse together on the couch, heads pitched back, sighing simultaneously.

"Thanks, by the way," she says.

"For what?"

"The bit about different races having children together and genetically improving the human race … dominant genes and all that … that was for me, wasn't it?"

The Statistician shrugs. "It's scientifically true."

And Hippie Avenger realizes something about The Statistician: As the Not-So-Super Friend with whom she has spent the least amount of time, he probably doesn't even know.

"You never met my parents, did you?"

He shakes his head no.

"So you didn't know that my mom is black and my dad is white."

"Really?" The Statistician says. "I thought you were Spanish, or Italian, or something like that." The Statistician's eyes meander from Hippie Avenger's shapely olive-bronze legs, to her long, curly black hair, then into her dark eyes. "Regardless, your parents passed some pretty good genes on to you."

This is the closest The Statistician has ever come to telling Hippie Avenger that he thinks she's beautiful.

Upstairs, the sounds of attempted conception begin yet again.

Hippie Avenger turns sideways, lays back, slides her toes under The Statistician's warm thigh once more, and wonders aloud, "Do you suppose there's a gene that makes them the way they are?"

The Statistician sighs. "Let's hope it's recessive."

THE ODDS

*"Sir, the possibility of successfully navigating an
asteroid field is approximately 3,720 to 1."
"Never tell me the odds."*

— Conversation between C-3PO and Han Solo,
from the movie *The Empire Strikes Back*, 1980

ADVENTURE SCORECARD: (Part One)
SUPER BATTLES!!!

SuperKen vs. Psycho Superstar

SuperKen once said, "I would have killed that little prick with my own bare hands," if Psycho Superstar hadn't been known to carry a switchblade. This statement was overheard by SuperBarbie, who found the remark to be in extremely poor taste, given that SuperKen made this bold declaration at Psycho Superstar's funeral. A heated argument ensued, which concluded in aggressive, angry sex on the reclining rear seat of the couple's Chrysler minivan.

WINNER: SuperKen

SuperBarbie vs. Miss Demeanor

When SuperBarbie tried to convince Miss Demeanor to join Teens Need Truth in order to help her "change her sinful ways," the resulting argument escalated into a full-scale brawl, from which both women emerged with cuts and bruises. SuperBarbie eventually apologized. Miss Demeanor did not. SuperKen became sexually aroused from watching the fight.

WINNER: SuperKen

The afternoon sun settles over the lake, and sunlight floods The Hall of Indifference. Hippie Avenger and The Statistician, drained from their scrap with The Perfect Pair, fall asleep together on the couch, in a pool of blood-warm light.

Neither The Perfect Pair's aggressive attempts at Creation upstairs, nor the laughing and screaming of Time Bomb and Miss Demeanor out in the lake, nor the rumble of The Drifter's Norton Commando rolling into the driveway wakes them. What rouses them from their cat like slumber is the gravelly voice of The Drifter demanding, "So what the hell has been going on here, anyway?"

He stands before the couch, still wearing his motorcycle jacket, holding his helmet against his hip like a gunslinger ready to draw. The Stunner stands behind him in a similar pose.

Oh no, thinks The Statistician. *He knows. She's told him!* He sits upright and yelps, "What? What do you mean?"

"Well," says The Drifter, sounding like Clint Eastwood in a Western movie, pointing ominously at the ceiling, "the two Co-Chairs of Teens Need Truth, who signed a friggin' *vow of chastity* in high school, are now screwing the bejeezus out of each other ten times a day. And they are *not* keeping it to themselves. Does that not seem a bit bizarro?"

He points out to the lake, through the sliding-glass door.

"And Miss Demeanor, who normally dresses like Elvira, Mistress of the Dark, is out there flouncing around in a pink bathing suit with a Miss Piggy decal on it. Bizarro. And Time Bomb is running around with her, wearing almost nothing, screaming and laughing. She usually never even smiles! I don't remember her smiling at your *wedding*, for crying out loud. Not even for the pictures. Is that not bizarro? And suddenly she's Miss Demeanor's best buddy? The one who once called her *Mizz Tight-Ass* to her face? Bizarro."

He crouches down before the couch.

"And here are you and Hippie Avenger, who I didn't think agreed on *anything*, snuggled up together like the last two kittens in the litter. So what the hell is going on around here? It's like I've landed on Bizarro World."

"Bizarro World?"

The Drifter breaks into a grin. "The alternate-universe planet in Superman comics, where everything is the opposite as it is on Earth."

"Bizarro World," The Statistician repeats.

"You should have read more comic books when you were a kid. Life wouldn't seem so weird."

The Drifter stands up, slides his arm around The Stunner's waist.

"Oh, by the way," The Stunner says flatly to The Statistician, "I told your brother about our past relationship."

The Statistician glares at The Stunner, as if to say, *I thought we had a deal.*

"No wonder you two were acting so weird around each other," The Drifter says. "You should have just *told* me that she used to be a student of yours. It's no big deal. It's not like you're grading her papers anymore, right?"

"Right."

"I mean, I know that would be unethical. But she's graduated, and she's got her degree now, so there's no conflict anymore, right?"

"No conflict. No."

"Actually," The Drifter says, "I think it's kind of cool that the two of you met before this weekend. I mean, what are the odds of that?"

"Well," says The Stunner, "in theoretical terms, taking the entire population of the Earth into account, the odds of any two people meeting are approximately, well … let's round it to seven billion to one. So the pure odds of any *two* humans meeting the same *third* human are about fourteen billion to one."

"But in *practical* terms," says The Statistician, looking her in the eyes for the first time since this morning, "you've got to take into account some geographic and demographic factors. You met at a Chinese place near the university, right?"

"Right."

"And my brother is staying at the university residence in the same area, correct?"

"Correct."

This exchange reminds The Stunner of the Socratic discussions she and The Statistician used to have in class, and later in his office, before that afternoon in her apartment.

"So," The Statistician says, "you can make the assumption that …"

The Stunner completes his sentence: "… that your sample group is limited to the average population of the University of Toronto campus and its surroundings."

She used to finish his thoughts this way during tutorial discussions. The other students were a bit jealous.

"So," says The Statistician, "give me a number."

"I … I don't have any data to work with. And there must be a thousand other variables involved."

"Sometimes you've got to ignore the thousand other variables and take an educated guess."

This sort of statement is one of the reasons that The Stunner was attracted to The Statistician; *academically* attracted to him, that is. He gave her permission to think past the numbers.

"Well, what's the population of Toronto?" she asks.

"The GTA is about five and half million. The city proper is about two and a half."

"So let's say the U of T and the Annex make up about a tenth of the actual city's area. Let's suppose the number of people in the defined area is about 250,000, then. So the odds of two brothers meeting the same girl at different times within roughly the same timeframe are about half a million to one."

"Pretty slim odds," The Statistician says, wearing that tight-lipped, difficult-to-interpret expression that attracted The Stunner to him in a *non-academic* way.

He had seemed so cool, so impermeable; she wanted to defrost him, to penetrate his shell. When she invited him up to her apartment, slipped him that note, touched his hand that certain way, looked him in the eyes with her Magnetic Power cranked up to Level Ten, she still figured that the odds of him actually showing up were also about a half million to one.

"But it happened anyway," she says, inspecting the toes of her riding boots. "Didn't it?"

"Indeed," says The Statistician. "It happened anyway."

The Drifter says, "You're both wrong. The odds were much lower than that."

"How so?" The Statistician and The Stunner say simultaneously.

"Well," The Drifter says, "maybe the odds of anyone meeting *randomly* are pretty high, but this wasn't random at all. You signed up for a *specific* math course that my brother *specifically* teaches. That made the odds of you meeting him much lower than random."

"Indeed," says The Statistician, nodding his head.

"And the odds of *me* meeting you were even better," the Drifter says to The Stunner.

"How so?" Only she says it this time.

"Because I was *looking* for you," The Drifter says. "I was looking for *you*. You in *particular*. And when you're looking for someone in particular, you're much more likely to find them."

The Stunner throws her arms around The Drifter's neck. "See? That's the kind of logic that makes me love you so much."

"I was looking for you," The Drifter says again, as if he's just solved the quadratic equation.

They turn and walk outside together.

The Statistician sighs. *I was looking for her, too.*

*

Hippie Avenger sits cross-legged on the couch, facing The Statistician. When she's sure that the Drifter and The Stunner have wandered far from the cottage, she says, "There's more to the story, isn't there?"

"She offered me sexual favours in exchange for a better grade," The Statistician says plainly. "And I accepted."

So he's not an android after all.

"I was her professor. And I'm married," he says. "I let my sexual frustrations outweigh my ethical obligations."

Hippie Avenger says, "I understand." And she does. She understands how it feels to want something — to want someone — that you're not supposed to have. She understands want, spelled-in-capital-letters *WANT*. She understands.

"It was irrational," he says. "It was weak."

She tries to lighten the mood. "Hey, it's not your fault. They say that God gave man both a brain and a penis, but only enough blood to operate one or the other."

The Statistician doesn't laugh. "You must think I'm a horrible person," he says.

"No. I just think you're a *person*."

She shuffles across the sofa, holds him just slightly longer than a friend comforting another friend should, just a decimal point past Platonic.

Then she resumes her cross-legged position on the couch, closer to him this time.

Upstairs, the Perfect Pair's bedposts begin to drum on the floorboards yet again.

Through the sliding glass door, The Statistician can see his wife splashing around in the water, laughing hysterically with Miss Demeanor, who just days earlier was her least favourite member of The Indifference League.

He can see The Drifter standing on the beach with The Stunner, holding her and kissing her. Just two weeks earlier, she was his Protégée. Now she's something else. And his younger brother has become something else, too.

"Every day that passes," The Statistician finally offers, "the world makes less sense to me."

"Bizarro World," Hippie Avenger says.

"Bizarro World, indeed."

SOLO

"I work alone."

— Superman, to Batman, from the
TV series *The Batman*, 2004–2008

Mr. Nice Guy applies the waterproof glue to the nylon patch and carefully places it over the leak on the rubber raft.

The English instructions that came with the Chinese-manufactured patch kit instruct: *"Importantly! To must allow correctly patch glue seal positively, dry approximate 15 minute to hold."*

Mr. Nice Guy interprets this correctly, and sets the timer on his Super G Digital Athletic Chronometer. When the beeper sounds, at exactly 4:11 p.m., he roots around in the shed for the foot-pump, but he can't find it anywhere. Rather than risk missing out on a raft ride with the happily stoned Miss Demeanor and the nearly naked Time Bomb, he drops to his knees and begins inflating the raft with air from his lungs. Then he tosses the plastic oars inside and carries the inflated boat to the water's edge, stumbling, dazed from oxygen deprivation.

"All right!" Miss Demeanor cheers. "Our hero!"

Mr. Nice Guy smiles dimly.

Time Bomb shoves the raft into the water, and her wet ass squeaks against the rubber as she slides in. Miss Demeanor climbs in after her, leans back, hangs her legs in the water over the inflated sidewalls, her legs spread wide.

Oh my God oh my God oh my God, thinks Mr. Nice Guy.

He kicks off his sandals and splashes into the lake. He doesn't have to take off his watch — the Super G is waterproof to fifty metres.

As he is about to climb in between them, Time Bomb says, "Girls only, buddy!"

"This is an exclusive cruise," Miss Demeanor says, "No Y-chromosomes allowed!"

"Ah," Mr. Nice Guy says. His mouth is dry and tastes like rubber. "Okay, then. Have fun."

They paddle out into the lake without him.

So, instead of bobbing up and down in a rubber vessel with two wet, scantily clad women, Mr. Nice Guy sets to work collecting sticks and dried leaves to use as starting fuel for tonight's bonfire.

He builds a multi-level tepee of branches and logs almost as tall as himself.

He drags the picnic tables down to the beach.

He arranges the lawn chairs around the fire pit.

He lugs coolers full of beer and ice down from the cottage.

Finally, as the sun is setting on the western horizon over the water, Mr. Nice Guy pauses to admire his work.

This will be the best bonfire ever witnessed at The Hall of Indifference.

Tonight's fire will roar like trapped spirits released.

The flames will reach up to the heavens.

This fire will be seen from space.

Just as he is about to strike the first match, a fat, cold raindrop strikes his cheek. He looks up. Dark, purple thunderclouds are rolling in. Lightning flashes in the distance.

There will be no bonfire tonight.

Oh well, he tells himself. *It's okay.*

He glances at his watch again. It reads 5:11 p.m.

Almost every time I look at my watch, there is an eleven on it. Almost every time. Weird.

He shrugs, and begins folding up the lawn chairs as the rain begins to fall.

It was a good day, anyway.

He is happy. All is well.

20

ORDER/
CHAOS

*"I'm an agent of chaos, and you know
the thing about chaos? It's fair."*

— The Joker, from the movie *The Dark Knight*, 2008

THE INDIFFERENCE LEAGUE

ADVENTURE SCORECARD: (Part Two)
SUPER BATTLES!!!

Mr. Nice Guy vs. SuperKen

SuperKen offends or humiliates Mr. Nice Guy in one way or another almost every time they encounter one another. One of these days, Mr. Nice Guy is going to make him pay for it. That day has not yet arrived.

WINNER: SuperKen

The Statistician vs. The Rest of the Indifference League

Whenever it rains at The Hall of Indifference, someone always drags out a board game. The Statistician has won 17 out of 17 Monopoly Games. He has won 4 out of 4 games of Risk. (SuperKen demanded rematches until the weekend was over.) He has won 3 out of 3 games of Scrabble. (Not necessarily because his vocabulary is better than any of the other Not-So-Superfriends, but because he always seems to maximize the numerical reward for any given word.) He has won 4 out of 5 Texas Hold 'Em tournaments. (The Statistician claims that the lone loss was due to "statistically unlikely hands", but The Drifter says it's because he knew The Statistician was bluffing …)

WINNER: Draw

19/20

At the huge, rough-hewn dining table inside The Hall of Indifference, The Statistician sits in one of the two chairs that still has its cushion intact, in order to avoid aggravating his bruises. Behind him, rain pecks at the windowpane.

Although SuperBarbie is not anxious to face The Statistician after their argument this afternoon, she sits across the table from him anyway, because that's where the only other chair with a cushion is; her own undercarriage is also bruised and sore from her War Hero's civilian population-growth mechanizations. SuperKen wheels in beside her, wearing the smirk of the satisfied.

The Drifter and The Stunner sit at the end of the table nearest the door, holding hands. The Statistician pulls out the chair beside him for Time Bomb, but rather than joining her husband, she takes a seat next to Miss Demeanor. So, Hippie Avenger takes the empty seat beside The Statistician instead.

Mr. Nice Guy opens the Monopoly game board at the centre of the table top, distributes bottles of beer and glasses of wine, and then doles out the pastel-coloured play-money. He wedges a chair in at the corner of the table, between Miss Demeanor and Hippie Avenger. And once again, the Not-So-Super Friends are all gathered around the dining-room table of The Hall of Indifference.

"Prepare to pick your playing pieces, people," Mr. Nice Guy playfully pontificates, the alliteration of the line causing him to spray spittle across the Monopoly board.

While Mr. Nice Guy wipes away the droplets with his sleeve, Hippie Avenger takes the piece shaped like a shaggy dog, like she always does. Nobody else wants the piece, anyway; as a symbol, it is the antithesis of financial success. And she would rather have a cute puppy than a race car or cannon, anyway.

Predictably, SuperKen grabs the battleship.

Miss Demeanor selects the boot, which reminds her of the Doc Martens she wore during her punk-rock days.

Time Bomb claims the horse and rider. She spent her pubescent summers at equestrian camp, which she attended not so much out of any great love for horses or sport, but because all the other girls in her neighbourhood were doing it, and because she looked pretty damned hot in those riding tights and tall boots. And she's feeling *very* hot today.

The Statistician reaches for the wheelbarrow, because he knows that he will inevitably be wheeling away everyone else's fake money at the end of the game.

The Stunner reaches for the wheelbarrow at the same time, believing it to be the one piece that no one else will want.

Her fingers touch The Statistician's. Both recoil.

Plump raindrops thump against the steel roof of The Hall of Indifference, like impatient fingers drumming on a desktop.

"You want the wheelbarrow?" she says. "You can have it."

"No, no," stammers The Statistician, "Please. You take it. I insist."

"You can have it."

"Take it. It's yours."

The Statistician instead plucks the top hat piece from the middle of the Monopoly board. He is not superstitious about which playing piece he uses. Such things are irrelevant to the mathematics involved. He can carry all their money away just as easily inside a top hat. He lays it open-end up on the GO square.

As far as is geometrically possible from The Statistician's top hat, The Stunner places her wheelbarrow on GO.

"That's the piece he always plays with," The Drifter whispers to The Stunner after she reluctantly picks up the wheelbarrow token, "You must have made quite an impression for him to give it up so easily."

Give it up so easily. The words ring in The Stunner's ears.

"Are you okay?" The Drifter says. "You're flushed."

"Just a bit warm," The Stunner says. "I'll take off my sweater."

The Statistician feels warm under the collar, too. He trained The Stunner. She could have earned that A+ without his help. She is the one person at the table who can make the calculations just as accurately as he can. It might simply come down to chance, now. Sweat beads on his forehead.

There is no motorcycle-shaped piece, so The Drifter takes the race car. This is usually the token that Mr. Nice Guy wants, so he reaches for the cannon instead, but SuperBarbie gets there first. Maybe she wants this replica piece of artillery to show her support for her soldier husband, but perhaps the big, round wheels and long barrel cocked upward remind her of something else she's been after lately.

"Looks like you get to choose between the iron and the thimble," SuperKen says to Mr. Nice Guy, in an effeminate voice. "Either way, you're doing the laundry, sweetie!"

Mr. Nice Guy was, in fact, washing everyone else's beach towels in the sink this afternoon, but he's miffed anyway.

"Well? Pick!" SuperKen squeals. "The thimble or the iron, honey?"

Hippie Avenger takes the thimble and places it open-end-up on the GO square.

"It's not a thimble," she says to SuperKen, "It's a pint glass. He told you he was a beer man."

Hippie Avenger smiles at Mr. Nice Guy, and pats him on the shoulder.

Maybe I do *still have a shot with her*, he thinks.

"Roll to see who goes first," Mr. Nice Guy says, throwing the dice across the table; when they tumble to a halt, one die shows five, and the other six. "Beat that!" he cries.

Everyone else rolls a lower number, except for The Statistician, who also rolls eleven.

"Tie breaker!" Mr. Nice guy says.

"It's okay," The Statistician answers. "I don't have to go first to win. I'll go *last* if that makes you happy."

"Tie breaker,' Mr. Nice Guy says again.

The Statistician shrugs and throws the dice again. Double sixes.

Mr. Nice Guy scoops the dice from the table, closes his eyes as he shakes them in his palm, throws again, opens his eyes. Another five and another six.

"What the hell is with all these elevens?"

"Two elevens," SuperKen says. "Big deal! It's not like the Cubs won the World Series."

"But I've been seeing elevens *everywhere* lately. Every time my stomach growls, it's 11:11 a.m. Every time I yawn and decide it's time for bed, it 11:11 p.m. Every other time I look at my watch, it's eleven minutes past the hour. I mean, is the universe trying to tell me something?"

The Statistician's eyes bug out. *"The universe?"*

"Well," Hippie Avenger says, "in numerology, the number eleven signifies …"

"Numerology?" The Statistician yelps.

"My parents were into it for a while."

"Peace, love, dope!" SuperKen grumbles.

"I didn't say that *I* was into it," Hippie Avenger says, glancing at The Statistician, but not at SuperKen. "Anyway, in numerology, the number eleven supposedly represents balance, since one is supposedly the purest of the numbers, and the numeral eleven is the combination of two ones."

She pauses for the expected interjection from The Statistician, but he doesn't say anything; he knows that she added the word "supposedly" for him. Twice.

"Hmm," says Miss Demeanor.

"What?" says Hippie Avenger.

"Well, when an alcoholic or a drug addict enters into a Twelve-Step Program, the eleventh step is the stage of balance and meditation. It fits with what the numerologists have to say, actually."

"Huh. Really." Hippie Avenger continues, "So, anyway," (she resists the urge to say "supposedly" again) "when the number eleven keeps appearing in your life, it's to encourage you to seek balance in your life, to right wrongs, to equalize work and play, thought and emotion, masculine and feminine …"

"He definitely needs to balance the masculine and feminine!" SuperKen snorts. "In fact, I think that you're on to something here. They give eleven-gun salutes to generals. There are eleven men on the field per team in football, soccer, and field hockey. And in rugby, the toughest game of 'em all, a regulation ball is eleven inches long. So maybe *the universe* is trying to tell you something, buddy — to grow a pair and be a fucking *man!*"

"Language, sweetie," SuperBarbie says.

The Statistician just shakes his head.

"Also," Hippie Avenger says, "the number eleven is a 'master number.' Ten is considered a perfect number, and eleven is one more than ten, so …"

"Ours go to eleven," The Drifter says, doing a perfect imitation of Nigel Tufnel.

"*This Is Spinal Tap!*" says Miss Demeanor. "Nice one, dude."

Mr. Nice Guy smiles. Eleven is better than ten. He *definitely* still has a shot with Hippie Avenger. "One more than perfect," he says.

The Statistician can't hold back any longer.

"How are the numerals ten or eleven more *perfect* than any of the others? Every number does an equally *perfect* job representing the quantity that it symbolizes."

"Well, *supposedly*," Hippie Avenger says, putting extra emphasis the word this time, "as a symbol, the two ones are perfectly parallel. Balance again. And, in numerology, there is some significance in the fact that eleven looks the same upside down as right side up."

"So does the number eight," The Statistician says.

"Your favourite number!" Hippie Avenger says. It takes her a moment to realize that the echo effect was caused by The Stunner saying exactly the same thing at almost exactly the same time.

Time Bomb's eyes narrow, and her lips tighten.

The Drifter clears his throat.

The Stunner quickly adds, "Zero also looks the same when flipped along a horizontal axis. In fact, it's the same with *any* number containing the digits zero, one, or eight. So it really doesn't mean anything." Then she nudges The Drifter and says, "Apollo *Eleven* was the first to land on the moon, though."

A slight grin cracks The Drifter's serious expression; she knows that he wanted to be an astronaut when he was a kid.

"*Ben Hur* won eleven Oscars," Miss Demeanor says, winking at The Drifter.

"So did *Titanic*," he adds.

"*M*A*S*H* — the TV series, not the movie — ran for *eleven seasons*." She winks again.

"So did *Cheers*! And, it had *eleven main characters*!"

"So did *M*A*S*H*!" Miss Demeanor licks her lips.

"We should go on a pop-culture quiz show together," The Drifter says.

"We would totally kick ass," Miss Demeanor says.

"We totally would," The Drifter affirms.

They punch knuckles across the table.

The Stunner frowns. *Did these two also have a thing together? Would he even tell me if they had?*

"Here's one," SuperKen says, "World War I ended on the eleventh hour of the eleventh day of the eleventh month of the year."

"You're all missing the point!" SuperBarbie says, suddenly animated, almost shouting. "Eleven is *not* a good number! It does *not* represent balance, or perfection, or anything like that. It's an *evil* number! Anyone remember *Nine-ELEVEN*? Anyone?"

"Oh, brother," The Statistician mutters.

"On September *eleventh*," SuperBarbie hisses, "terrorists flew an airplane, *Flight number eleven*, into the Twin Towers, which, side by side, look like the *number eleven*! The next plane to hit the towers was Flight seventy-seven. Seventy-seven can be divided evenly … by *eleven*!" She turns to Mr. Nice Guy. "So, if you're seeing elevens everywhere, it's a sign that something *terrible* is going to happen!"

Mr. Nice Guy stammers, "But, um, but …"

"There is no real meaning in any of that," The Statistician says, in his full professorial tone. "There is no correlation between the number eleven and anything that happened on that terrible day."

"The Twin Towers had 110 storeys each! Divided by ten, that's *eleven*! Flight eleven had 92 passengers. Nine plus two equals *eleven*! Flight 77 had 65 passengers. Six plus five equals *eleven*!"

"Well, actually," SuperKen says, "Flight 77 had sixty-*four* passengers …"

"You were *hurt* fighting the people that did this!" Super-Barbie barks. "You've been *fighting* the evil that began on that day! Eleven is an *evil* number!"

"Well, okay, but …"

"'New York City' has eleven letters!" she cries. "'Afghan-istan' has eleven letters! 'The Pentagon' has eleven letters! All of this on the Internet! It's right there for anyone to see!"

"'It's bullshit' has eleven letters, too," says The Statistician. "I also read *that* on the Internet."

"Nine-eleven is our telephone code for an emergency," SuperBarbie says. "Do you know what their telephone area code is?" She doesn't wait for a response. "It's *eleven-nine*! Try to tell me *that's* a coincidence."

"It is indeed a coincidence. There is no meaning in any of it."

SuperbBarbie is filling her lungs to dispense more examples of evil elevens, but The Statistician continues.

"Let me illustrate," he says. "Take the ones from the elevens in September eleventh, Flight 11, and so on. One plus one equals two. Is *two* therefore an evil number? There were obviously two Twin Towers. Two airplanes hit them. The airplanes each had two wings. Everyone involved had two arms, two legs, two eyes, two ears. *Everyone* involved. Is *everyone* therefore evil?"

He turns to Mr. Nice Guy.

"I hope you haven't also been seeing the number *two* everywhere. That would be *really* bad news from the universe."

Mr. Nice Guy doesn't laugh.

The Statistician sighs.

"People have a hard time dealing with how randomly things in the universe tend to happen, the chaos of it all. Even *I* have a difficult time getting my brain around it sometimes. So we try to find *order* in the chaos. Sometimes we actually *find* it. We call that science. Other times, when we can't find the order, we *invent* one, and *impose* it upon the chaos. It's the reason that …" his voice trails off.

"It's the reason that *what*?" SuperBarbie says.

He was going to say, *It's the reason that so many people believe in things like numerology. Or astrology. Or God.*

For some reason, though, he stopped himself. Or something stopped *him*.

He shakes his head. *I stopped myself.*

"People wouldn't have to invent explanations for the things that happen in the world, if only we had more …"

He pauses. He can't recall the word he wants to use. This almost never happens to The Statistician.

He repeats, "If only we had more …"

"Prayer," says SuperBarbie.

"Control," says SuperKen.

"Freedom," says Hippie Avenger.

"Experience," says The Drifter.

"Forgiveness," says The Stunner.

"Anarchy!" says Miss Demeanor.

Mr. Nice Guy mumbles, "Love."

The Statistician shakes his head. He will never remember the word now.

"None of those things," he says. "Or maybe all of them. I don't know."

Mr. Nice Guy glances down at his Super G Chronometer. The bold, black digits on its LCD display read 9:11 p.m.

"Hey," Time Bomb says, "I've got one! The Indifference League has had *eleven* members in total. Well, that's if you include Psycho Superstar and Sweetie Pie."

Mr. Nice Guy blinks. Still 9:11.

The Statistician says, "Let's just play Monopoly now, okay?"

"If you don't include them, though," Time Bomb continues, her penciled eyebrows arched high, "there are just nine of us. Nine-eleven! Spooky."

Mr. Nice Guy closes his eyes. When he opens them, his watch still reads 9:11.

It doesn't mean anything. It doesn't mean anything. It doesn't mean anything.

The Statistician reiterates, "Let's just play Monopoly now."

The display on Mr. Nice Guy's chronometer blinks, changes to 9:12. He starts breathing again.

The Statistician reaches for the dice.

21

WORLD DOMINATION

*"World domination. The same old dream. Our asylums
are full of people who think they're Napoleon. Or God."*

— JAMES BOND, AGENT 007, FROM THE MOVIE *DR. NO*, 1962

ADVENTURE SCORECARD: (Part Three)
SUPER BATTLES!!!

The Statistician vs. The Drifter

These SuperBrothers have had many arguments over the years, and usually, The Statistician's "reason over emotion" debating tactics have won. The few physical altercations were also almost always won by The Statistician, up until The Drifter's growth spurt at age fifteen, when he decisively beat The Statistician in a fistfight. Since then, there has been an uneasy truce between The Drifter and The Statistician.

WINNER: Draw

The Statistician vs. The Perfect Pair

There have been dozens of arguments over the years: Pro-Choice vs. Pro-Life, Evolution vs. Creation, Batman vs. Spider-Man … The Statistician always knows he has won, and The Perfect pair always believe that they have won.

WINNER: Draw

20/20

The Statistician always wins at Monopoly. He has never lost.

The other members of The Indifference League compete to see who will be bankrupted last, which hero among them will hold out the longest against The Statistician's endlessly calculating brain.

The Statistician's strategy is based entirely on mathematical formulae and probabilities. Early in the game, he will try to acquire all four of the railroads, since owned together they provide the largest payback for the smallest early investment. Later he'll trade them away for properties he needs to complete his groups of same-coloured properties, so he can start buying houses with his accumulated "railroad fares." He always buys exactly three houses for each property, as he has calculated that this provides the highest investment-to-rent-intake ratio.

He will try to own all three properties in the orange group (New York Avenue, Tennessee Avenue, and St. James Place) since, based on the statistical permutations of die rolls between two and twelve, they are the properties with the highest collective likelihood of being landed upon by opponents. As he collects more theoretical money, he will then attempt to procure the red and yellow properties, which are second and third most likely to be landed upon by other players. And so on, until he wins the game.

Mr. Nice Guy is always the first player to go bankrupt. He lets people land on his properties without making them pay rent. He will accept whatever property trades he's offered, with no haggling. Sometimes he will *give* a property away just because one of the others needs it to complete a colour group. You can't win the game when you play like that.

Time Bomb spends Monopoly money with wanton abandon, just like she does with real money in real life. She buys every property she lands on, including the nearly worthless Electric Company and Waterworks, in the same way that she once bought a handbag for four thousand dollars, which she's used exactly once. Unlike in real life, though, Time Bomb does not have access to her father's endless supply of tobacco money, so she is usually the second player to go bankrupt.

In previous games, The Statistician's final opponent has been either SuperKen, who can be quite aggressive when negotiating property trades, or Miss Demeanor, who saves her money and waits until Mr. Nice Guy goes bankrupt so she can buy his mortgaged properties at a discount, or Hippie Avenger, who repeatedly throws advantageous dice rolls which defy mathematical probability.

*

They are an hour into the game now. There are a dozen empty beer bottles on the table, and three empty bottles of wine.

All of the properties have been purchased, and phase two of the Statistician's campaign for simulated capitalistic victory has begun.

The game so far has played out even better than usual for The Statistician; he has been lucky enough to procure his desired orange and red properties simply by rolling the dice fortuitously and landing on them first, and he gets the yellow properties in an even trade with Mr. Nice Guy for his railroads (which, while valuable in the first half of the game, are less so once the houses and hotels start going up). The Statistician immediately buys three houses each for his newly acquired properties.

On Mr. Nice Guy's next turn, he lands on Atlantic Avenue, which he just traded to The Statistician. His next roll is a two and a one, which lands him on Marvin Gardens, the final of his former yellow properties. Mr. Nice Guy is bankrupted without anyone ever taking a ride on his newly acquired railroads.

The Statistician shakes his head in disbelief. "The odds of you making two successive rolls of two dice and landing on two properties within three squares of each other, within exactly two turns of you trading them to another player, are …"

"Are not as high as you might think," The Stunner says. "The odds are exactly thirty-six to one."

The Statistician raises an eyebrow. "How do you figure?"

"Six times six," The Stunner says. "It's only the odds of casting any one number out of six, times the odds of casting any other one number out of six. The other factors are irrelevant."

"Good logic," The Statistician says, "but slightly flawed. On *two* dice, you can roll either a one and a two, or a two and a one, to get a total of three. So the probability of rolling a three on two dice is *two* chances in thirty-six, or *eighteen* to one."

The Stunner slaps her forehead. "Uh! How did I miss that!"

"An A+ for the effort, though," The Statistician says to his Protégée.

An A+ for the effort. Their cheeks flush red and they both stop laughing.

"You're blushing again," The Drifter says to The Stunner.

A roll of thunder rattles the windowpane in the living room of The Hall of Indifference.

"One divided by eighteen still equals *loser*," SuperKen says to Mr. Nice Guy.

Mr. Nice Guy shrugs and says, "Oh, well. Not everyone gets to win."

He retreats into the kitchen to put some late-night snacks in the oven, and to wash up the dishes from dinner.

"Loser!" SuperKen coughs as Mr. Nice Guy walks away.

"Why do you have to be such a jerk?" Hippie Avenger says to SuperKen.

"Peace, love, dope!" SuperKen snipes at her, flashing the peace sign as if he's giving her the finger. *"One Race! The Human Race!"*

"Honey!" SuperBarbie says, "Don't be so aggressive. It's like you've been possessed by Jake!"

She regrets saying this even before the words have finished tumbling out of her mouth.

SuperKen says, "Don't *ever* compare me to that asshole!"

"Don't *ever* call him an asshole!" Miss Demeanor says. "Jake may have been a little rough around the edges. He may have been a bit hyperactive. He may have even taken the name of the Lord in vain once or twice. But he wasn't homophobic."

"He wasn't racist, either," Hippie Avenger adds.

"And he never put down his friends to make himself feel bigger," Miss Demeanor says.

"Yeah, he was a real saint, a real stand-up kind of guy, wasn't he?" SuperKen says. "Except that he didn't know enough to keep his hands off other people's girlfriends, did he?"

SuperBarbie blushes. "Now, honey, you know you over-reacted to that. There was never anything going on between me and …"

"I saw what I saw," SuperKen says. "And that prick wasn't so cool or so tough when I got finished with him, was he? He was nobody's goddamn lover boy then, was he?"

He sticks his jaw out at SuperBarbie, waiting for her to admonish him for his very blatant taking-of-the-Lord's-name-in-vain. She doesn't say anything.

Mr. Nice Guy can hardly believe what he's hearing. Psycho Superstar definitely had sex with Miss Demeanor, and probably also with Hippie Avenger, but he fooled around with SuperBarbie, too? *Damn! What was his secret?*

"Let's just play the stupid game," SuperKen says.

SuperKen's Monopoly strategy is to invest aggressively in hotels for his properties, as early as possible in the game, sometimes even mortgaging one property to develop another. When The Statistician helpfully suggests that he might run into cash-flow problems later, SuperKen responds by barking, "Strike first, strike hard!"

When he is the next player to go bankrupt, SuperBarbie, The Drifter, and The Stunner vote to allow him to "merge his assets" with SuperBarbie, while Hippie Avenger, Miss Demeanor, and The Statistician vote against it. The deciding vote is given to Mr. Nice Guy upon his return from the kitchen.

"No hard feelings, eh, buddy?" SuperKen says.

So Mr. Nice Guy votes for the merger, which is short-lived anyway. Within six turns, SuperKen's "deficit financing strategy" leaves The Perfect Pair without any joint assets left on the table.

"Oh, well," chirps SuperBarbie, "it's only a game, y'know. Honey, would you come upstairs for a minute and help me with something?"

After a lengthy pit stop in the washroom, SuperKen obliges. The next baby-making session is going to be *quite* aggressive.

*

Another hour passes. There are now twenty-six empty beer bottles on the table, and seven empty bottles of wine.

The Perfect Pair are still upstairs, behind closed bedroom doors. The hiss of the rainfall does not completely drown out the even-louder-than-usual sounds of their copulation.

The remaining active Monopoly players are The Statistician, The Stunner, and Miss Demeanor.

Hippie Avenger was knocked out of the game by Miss Demeanor, who did a little victory dance while Time Bomb cheered, "Go girl! Go girl! Go girl!" over and over and over again. They slapped each other's palms in the air, over-celebrating her defeat just like those Varsity Sports Bitches in high school used to do. So Hippie Avenger is quietly hoping that The Statistician will win the game like he always does.

The Drifter, Time Bomb, and Mr. Nice Guy, all of whom were bankrupted by The Statistician, are silently rooting against him.

Miss Demeanor is about to roll the dice when The Statistician notices that her boot has been parked on his Illinois Avenue property for the past round.

"Not so fast!" he intones, "First you owe me some rent for your stay in one of my three lovely green houses … seven-hundred-and-fifty dollars, to be exact."

"Sorry," Miss Demeanor says. "My bad."

"Your bad *what?*" The Statistician says, with that professorial tone in his voice. "Perhaps what you mean to say is, 'Sorry, my mistake.' I'm surprised that someone with your excellent education you would use a grammatically incorrect phrase like that."

Miss Demeanor's eyebrows arch upward, and her eyes widen. "And I'm surprised that someone with your impeccable upbringing would attempt to humiliate another person over something as trivial as the use of an idiomatic colloquialism."

Miss Demeanor has just said what each of the other Not-So-Super Friends has wanted to say to The Statistician at one time or another, only better.

Time Bomb cheers for her new ally. "Yes! I hate it when he does that to me."

You also hate a lot of other things I try to do to you, is what The Statistician wants to say. Instead, he mutters to Miss Demeanor, "Sorry. You're right. My bad." He doesn't want to lose the game for the first time ever because he's given the others a non-game-related reason to team up against him. "I'll let you go rent-free this time, okay?"

Miss Demeanor's eyes narrow, and she flips several pastel-coloured bits of fake currency across the board at The Statistician.

"I don't need your charity," she says, "because you certainly won't be getting mine when you stay at my hotel on the Boardwalk."

"That's telling him, girlfriend!" Time Bomb cheers, high-fiving Miss Demeanor.

"What the hell has gotten into you?" The Statistician splutters.

"'*Gotten*'?" Time Bomb says, "'*Gotten*'? Is it grammatically correct to say '*gotten*'?"

"Seriously," The Statistician says, "what has gotten into you today?"

Time Bomb puts her fists on her hips. "Well, I'll tell you one thing that ain't gettin' into me tonight, mister, and that's you!"

"Where is this coming from?" The Statistician demands, eyeing Miss Demeanor.

"Bankrupt *me*, will ya!" Time Bomb huffs.

"What?" The Statistician yelps. "But … that's just the way the game works."

"You have *no idea* how the game works," Time Bomb says coolly.

Miss Demeanor shakes the dice and gets Time Bomb to blow on them. "For luck," she says.

She lands on B&O Railroad, the one square between The Statistician's bankruptcy-causing red and yellow properties.

"Lucky, indeed," The Statistician says.

Outside The Hall of Indifference, there is a distant flash of white lightning, followed seconds later by a rumbling roll of thunder.

"I've got a wager for you," Miss Demeanor says to The Statistician. "If I bankrupt you before you bankrupt me, I get to take your wife into the city to get a tattoo of Wilma Flintstone on her butt."

"What? Why? What does this have to do with the game?"

"It has *everything* to do with the game," Time Bomb says, downing the last gulp from her wineglass, pouring more for herself and Miss Demeanor.

"But what about your *dermatological sensitivities*?" The Statistician says.

"It's my ass. I can do what I want with it."

"Fine," says The Statistician, to both his wife and Miss Demeanor. "You're on."

The Drifter leans forward on his elbows, staring with smoldering eyes at The Statistician, then at The Stunner, then at his brother again. "If we're betting on the game, then I've got a wager for you too, big brother. If you go bankrupt before my girlfriend does, I get to ask you one question. And you have to answer it. Truthfully."

"But sweetie," The Stunner says, "It's a bad bet. I can't beat him. He knows all the odds. He knows all the variables. He knows all the permutations."

"And so do you," The Drifter says. "Roll the dice."

"Wait," Hippie Avenger says, understanding what is now at stake. "What does he get if he wins?" She turns to The Statistician. "What do you want if you win?"

The Statistician closes his eyes.

What I don't *want is for my wife to get some crass tattoo carved onto her tenth-percentile ass, but that's what she's going to do, whether I like it or not.*

What I don't *want is for my brother or my wife to know what happened between my Protégée and me, but that's what he's going to ask me about.*

When The Statistician opens his eyes again, Hippie Avenger is the first person he sees.

And what I do want, I know I can't have.

There is a blinding flash of lightning and an immediate, ear-ringing crack of thunder.

The lights in the cottage dim for a moment, but they don't go out.

The Statistician stands up and begins dividing his pastel-coloured play-money between Miss Demeanor and The Stunner.

"What are you doing?" Miss Demeanor demands.

"I can't win," The Statistician says, dealing the cardboard deeds to his theoretical properties between Miss Demeanor and The Stunner like playing cards.

"Go get your tattoo," he says to Time Bomb, "if that's what you want to do. It's your body. And you've got all the real money, and you hold all the real deeds. So do whatever you want to. I can't stop you."

"Well, all right!" Miss Demeanor cheers, raising her hands for another high-five from Time Bomb. "Let's get you branded, baby!"

Time Bomb slaps palms with Miss Demeanor, but with less enthusiasm than before.

"Well, let's go," Miss Demeanor says, "before you chicken out."

"Tonight?"

"Hell yeah, tonight! I know this twenty-four hour parlour, best needle artist in the city. She did almost all of mine!" Miss Demeanor turns to The Statistician. "Don't worry, Daddy, I'll have her home by sunrise."

As they rush out into the rain, Time Bomb turns to The Statistician and says, "See you later," almost like she's asking a question.

"Yeah. See you later."

The Statistician sits down again at the table, folds his hands where his stack of phony deeds and cash had been, and faces his younger brother.

Rain blasts against the steel roof over their heads, rumbling like a volcano about to erupt.

"Okay, then," The Statistician says, locking his eyes onto the Drifter's. He doesn't blink. Nothing moves but his mouth. "Ask."

The Drifter hesitates. He knows The Statistician better than anyone. He knows that if he doesn't phrase this in exactly the right way, his brother will calculate a way to evade the question.

"You two are still being weird around each other," The Drifter says, "and, well, I just can't help wondering … did your … relationship … go beyond the limits … the accepted boundaries … of a normal student-teacher relationship?"

"Yes," The Statistician says. "Yes. It did."

The Stunner's eyes are wide and dark.

"I was attracted to her. I made a proposition. I offered to give her an A+ grade in exchange for … well, you know."

The Drifter's fists clench.

"She said no," The Statistician says, looking his brother in the eyes, not even blinking. "She turned me down. And even though I graded her twice as hard as the other students, she earned the A+ anyway."

"Well, at least I know you're telling the truth," The Drifter says, the muscles in his cheeks twitching. "You never look anyone in the eyes when you're lying."

"She wasn't looking for a man like me," The Statistician says. "She was looking for a man like you."

The Drifter has wanted to beat his older brother at something, at anything, since they were little kids. Now he feels like he might cry.

The Stunner is crying. Her tears splash on the plastic tablecloth.

The Drifter puts his arms around The Stunner. "I'm sorry," he says. "I needed to hear it from him."

"I hope you can forgive me some day," The Statistician says.

The Stunner cries even harder.

Rain hisses against the ground outside.

"Tonight is kind of like the night we met," The Drifter says to The Stunner. "Want to go out and relive the ride?"

"Fraser," The Stunner says to The Drifter, "Can we just ride all night? And not come back here?"

"Sure, Cassie," he tells her. "We'll ride all night. Let's go."

*

Hippie Avenger and Mr. Nice Guy sit at the table with The Statistician, unsure of what to do or say next. Mr. Nice Guy is desperate to break the storm-punctuated tension. He is equally desperate to engineer a moment alone with Hippie Avenger. It's the final night of the long weekend. It's now or never.

He leans over and whispers to her, "Why don't you and I drive into town, grab a drink somewhere. I'm sure he could use some time alone right now."

"I'm okay," The Statistician says.

"I think I'll just turn in for the night," Hippie Avenger says. She leans over and kisses The Statistician on the cheek. "Good night, mister," she says.

As Hippie Avenger climbs the stairs, Mr. Nice Guy stretches, forces a yawn, and says, "Well, I'm pretty beat, too."

Maybe I should go get my *goodnight kiss*, he thinks. By the time Mr. Nice Guy is upstairs, though, the door to Hippie Avenger's room is closed.

*

Alone at the table, The Statistician gathers the money and the deeds, and puts them in their respective slots inside the game box. Then he plucks the pieces from the Monopoly board: the top hat, which he had never worn until tonight. The Stunner's wheelbarrow, which was never really his in the first place. Miss Demeanor's boot, which certainly kicked some ass this evening. He tosses the little metallic tokens into the box with The Perfect Pair's battleship and cannon, The Drifter's race car, Time Bomb's horse and rider, Mr. Nice Guy's thimble, and Hippie Avenger's shaggy dog.

He folds the game board, places the lid of the box over-top, and sits alone at the table. Behind his bruised back, rain pecks gently at the windowpane.

The Statistician had always won at Monopoly. He had never lost.

22

CODE OF ETHICS

"With great power comes great responsibility."

— UNCLE BEN TO PETER PARKER (A.K.A. SPIDER-MAN),
FROM THE MOVIE *SPIDER-MAN*, 2002

t is not the otherworldly scent of The Stunner's lovingly blended coffee that rouses The Statistician from sleep this morning. The Stunner and The Drifter did not return last night. Today they are on the road somewhere together, moving farther and farther away from The Hall of Indifference.

What jolts The Statistician awake today is the pungent essence of rubbing alcohol and antibiotic lotion. It burns his nostrils and eyes.

Time Bomb is bent over the chair where she's set her overstuffed, name-brand-of-the-month cosmetic bag. She's rummaging frantically though its contents.

"Damn it," she says. "I was sure I brought a tube of …"

She is naked from the waist down. Upon her right butt cheek is a three-inch tattoo of Wilma Flintstone. The skin around Wilma is swollen and irritated.

When she notices that her husband is awake, Time Bomb says, "Hey, hi." She arches her back, sticks her ass out, and says in her rare flirtatious voice, "So … what do you think?"

Despite The Statistician's distaste for tattoos, his penis immediately rises to Red Alert status. It's been so long since he's seen his wife in this position. Their honeymoon was the last time.

"Yabba-dabba-doo!" he says, slipping out from under the covers, dropping his pajama pants on the floor. He advances, grips her waist just above the hips, centres himself behind her.

She leaps away from him, spins around, and yelps "Are you crazy? Get that dirty thing away from me! Do you want me to get an infection?"

"I just … I was … I just thought …"

"I need some more antibiotic cream," Time Bomb says, any trace of flirtation now erased from her voice. "Go into town and get me some, okay? And some rubbing alcohol, too."

"Are you coming with me?"

She slides onto the bed, lying on her stomach.

"Bouncing over the back roads won't be the most enjoyable experience for me at the moment."

The Statistician sighs and reaches for his pants.

"Okay. See you later, then."

Wilma Flintstone smiles smugly at The Statistician as he closes the bedroom door behind him.

*

Behind another closed bedroom door, SuperKen is looking at SuperBarbie's naked body. She is curled up in a tight ball on the floor, hugging her knees to her chest, sobbing so violently that she's almost hyperventilating.

Beside her on the rug is a paper cup half-filled with her own urine, and the wand from yet another pregnancy testing kit. No blue line has appeared on the wand. SuperBarbie is still not pregnant.

SuperKen knows that the right strategic move in this volatile situation would be to kneel down beside her, rub her back, stroke her hair, and comfort her, but his rigid leg braces prevent him from doing this, so he just drags the wheelchair over and sits beside her.

"Hey, come on," SuperKen says, "why don't we just try again?"

"Pointless!" she gasps. "It's pointless!"

"Aw, come on, sweetie. Come on, now."

"Just go. Just go away. I want to be alone now."

He leans forward as far as he can, reaches out to touch her.

She swats his hand away.

"Go. Now."

SuperKen shrugs, stands up from the wheelchair, and limps out of the bedroom. He takes one last look at his naked wife before pushing the door shut.

A good soldier knows when it's time to retreat.

*

The Statistician rolls down the driver's-side window of Hippie Avenger's VW Microbus and hangs his right arm outside. Cool, damp air from last night's storm rushes around his face and neck. Wet gravel hisses beneath the spinning tires.

He wishes that Hippie Avenger had come along for the ride, but she wanted to take a bath "before the morning bathroom rush hour."

The Statistician vaguely remembers an old-fashioned drugstore in the one-stoplight town near Mr. Nice Guy's cottage. He hopes it will be open on a holiday Monday; he doesn't relish the idea of having to drive all the way back to the city to get a salve for Time Bomb's I'll-show-you-who's-boss tattoo.

He wheels the Microbus up to the curb beside The Village Apothecary. A hand-lettered sign in the bay window announces, YEP, WE'RE OPEN, FOLKS!

Inside the cluttered, musty shop, a lanky young man with an unkempt red beard struggles to hoist multi-roll packages of toilet paper onto a shelf above his head. The job is made more difficult by the fact that he is missing his right arm at the elbow.

"Here," The Statistician offers, "let me help you with that."

"I don't need any help," he snaps. "I can do it myself."

At the back of the narrow shop, perched atop a rickety stool, a heavy-set woman in a pink track suit admonishes,

"Don't take it out on the customers, Stevie." Then she says to The Statistician, "He hasn't been in much of a mood since he got back from overseas."

"Oh?" The Statistician says, to the boy, not to the woman. "Where did you go?"

"Vacation in Afghanistan," Stevie says, waving his stump in the air.

"He did us proud," his mother beams. "He got hit while he was dragging fallen men out of the line of fire."

"No big deal," Stevie says. "Any one of the other guys woulda done the same thing for me."

"It *was* a big deal. He's being awarded the Star of Military Valour."

"Mommmmmmmm!"

"Hey, one of my friends was injured over there, too," The Statistician says.

"Oh yeah?" the kid says. "What's his name?"

When The Statistician mentions SuperKen, Stevie drops a package of toilet paper on the floorboards.

"You gotta be friggin' kidding me! You know *OC Douchebag*?"

"Stevie!" the woman yelps. "Watch your language!"

"But, Mom! Remember the guy I told you about? That quarter-inch admiral who was always giving the big inspirational speeches about …"

"About the time his basketball team was down by ten?" Stevie's mom says, jumping up from her stool. "And how they all pulled together in the final minutes to win the championship?"

The Statistician has heard that story many times himself. SuperKen had dunked the basket that won the game, of course.

"That's the guy!" Stevie says. "OC Douchebag!"

His mother doesn't correct him this time. Instead, she chortles, "The *Parachutist*!"

"No, it's not the same guy, then," The Statistician says. "My friend is in the infantry, I think. Definitely not the Air Force."

"Nah," Stevie laughs, "We just *call* him The Parachutist. After what happened, you know."

"No, I *don't* know. What happened?"

Stevie glances at his mother, then at The Statistician, then back at his mother again. "Well, if he's your friend, I probably shouldn't …"

"Please?" The Statistician says.

"Oh, I don't know," Stevie says. "You're his buddy and all. So, like, what exactly did he tell you?"

"He said that neither Aerial Ordnance, nor Improvised Explosive Devices, nor Area Denial Munitions were factors in his injury. Or something like that."

"Well, he's right, they weren't."

"He said he wasn't at liberty to discuss it."

"Well, I'm not sure that's true," Stevie says, "but I can understand him not wanting anybody to know about it."

"So what happened?"

Stevie glances again at his mother again. She shrugs and nods.

"Well," he says, "we were on the transport plane, right? A C-130 Hercules. One big-assed plane, eh? Anyway, we had just set down on the airstrip, and OC Douche … your buddy, well, he decides to give this rousing speech about how God's on our side, that we're fighting the good fight, going after the infidels, et cetera, et cetera. Well, nobody's really listening, and the commander's looking at some maps up front. Well, normally on a Hercules you just wait for the rear cargo door to open before disembarking, right?"

"Sure, right," The Statistician says, as if he knows a C-130 Hercules from the *Millennium Falcon*.

"Anyway," Stevie continues, "the OC gets himself all charged up, throws the side hatch open, and charges right outta the plane, hollering, 'Follow me, boys! Follow me!'"

232 · RICHARD SCARSBROOK

It sounds to The Statistician like something that the Male Athlete of the Year would do.

Stevie kneels to pick up the fallen package of toilet paper. It's tricky with just one hand, but he manages it.

"Like I said," he continues, "the Hercules is a big-assed plane. And you normally exit out the back, so there was no ladder or steps or anything at the side hatch. The OC fell all the way down. Smashed his legs up real good."

"No medal for him, I guess," Stevie's mom says.

"Probably not," Stevie says, as he leaps in the air and tosses the bundle of toilet paper up onto the top shelf, like a basketball star sinking the winning basket.

*

When The Statistician arrives back at the cottage, SuperKen is sitting on the front steps outside.

"Hi there, OC," The Statistician says.

"Hi … hey, did you just call me OC?"

"That's your rank, isn't it?"

"Well, yeah, but …"

"At the drugstore up the road, I met a kid who served with you in Afghanistan."

SuperKen's eyes widen. *Play it cool,* he tells himself. *Play it cool. A good soldier never shows fear in the face of the enemy.*

"Oh, yeah? And what was this soldier's name?"

"His mother called him Stevie. He didn't look to be more than twenty."

"Tall, skinny kid? Red hair?"

"That's him."

"Private Steven James. Good kid. Good soldier. How's he doing?"

"He's missing an arm from the elbow down."

SuperKen's face turns white. "Oh," he says. "I didn't know. Oh."

"He was restocking the shelves. He didn't want any help."

"Good for him. Good for him."

The brown paper bag containing antibiotic cream and rubbing alcohol for Time Bomb swings back and forth in The Statistician's right hand.

The index fingernail of SuperKen's right hand taps arhythmically on one of his titanium leg braces.

Finally, SuperKen says, "I suppose you're going to tell everyone."

"No. I'm not going to tell everyone."

SuperKen thinks of SuperBarbie, naked and sobbing on the floor upstairs.

"I suppose you're going to tell my wife, though."

"No, I'm not going to tell her," The Statistician says. "But *you* probably should."

SuperKen sticks out his jaw. "And are *you* going to tell *your* wife that you fooled around with your brother's girl-friend while she was still your student?"

"I … you … how …?"

"I'm not a math prodigy," SuperKen says, "but I can put two and two together."

The Statistician straightens.

"Yes. Yes, I'm going to tell her. She's going to find out sooner or later, and I'd rather that it was from me."

The Statistician steps around SuperKen, up the stairs and into the cottage.

"As a matter of fact, I'm going to go tell her right now."

SuperKen says under his breath, "You're a real hero."

BE IT KNOWN THAT, ON BEHALF OF
HER MAJESTY THE QUEEN OF CANADA,
THE GOVERNOR GENERAL
HAS AWARDED

THE STAR OF MILITARY VALOUR

TO

PRIVATE STEVEN JAMES,
SMV, SM, AND GCS-SWA
WIARTON, ONTARIO

*

Amidst chaos and under sustained and intense enemy fire in
Afghanistan, Private James selflessly and repeatedly exposed
himself to great peril in order to assist his wounded comrades.

Even after being severely injured, he continued to move
immobilized personnel to safety. His valiant conduct saved
the lives of many members of his company.

BIZARRO
WORLD

"Us do opposite of all Earthly things!"

— BIZARRO (THE "OPPOSITE" SUPERMAN),
FROM *ADVENTURE COMICS*, 1961

The Statistician leaves SuperKen outside on the front steps of the cottage. Inside, he strides past the closed bathroom door, past the empty dining table, around the sofa in the living room, and up the stairs that he tumbled down just yesterday morning.

He is going to tell his wife the truth. He is going to ask her to forgive him. He is going to ask her if maybe they can start again.

When he reaches the top of the staircase, though, three of the four bedroom doors are wide open, including the one he is sharing with Time Bomb. She's not there. The zippered plastic bag that her tiny bikini came inside, labelled *Wicked Weasel*, is empty on the bed. Her beach towel is missing, also.

Miss Demeanor and Mr. Nice Guy are gone, too. Perhaps Mr. Nice Guy has convinced them to take him on the raft ride he missed out on yesterday.

The Statistician descends the stairs and waits in the living room. When his wife returns, he will tell her everything. It cannot go on like this any longer.

*

Outside, a sunbeam breaks through the clouds. Inside, intense white light streams through the window and onto the floor where SuperBarbie lies, curled up, naked, sniffling, and gasping.

When she feels the warmth of the sunlight on her skin, she stops crying. She kneels on the floor, illuminated.

She closes her eyes, folds her hands together, and prays out loud.

"Please God, please. I want to be a mother more than anything in the world. My baby cries out to me in my dreams, 'I'm waiting, Mommy, I'm waiting!' Please, Lord, bring my baby to me. Please. I can withstand anything else, but I need my baby now."

When she opens her eyes again, the sun is once again hidden behind a curtain of cloud.

*

Hippie Avenger lays back in the antique oval tub, surrounded by steaming, oil-scented water. She feels slippery and sexy. She presses her knees against either wall of the wide bathtub, curls her toes around the *X*-shaped hot and cold water taps. She snakes the middle finger of her right hand through her wet tangle of pubic hair, and submerges the Purple Pal in the grip of her left hand.

She hums along with the sounds of the submerged vibrator humming, "Mmmmmmm," and is grateful that she spent the extra money on the waterproof model.

She bites down on her bottom lip to keep from screaming out loud.

"Mmmmm, mmmmmmMMMMMMMmmmmmmmm, *mmMMMMMMMMMMMmmmm*," she moans, as her feet twitch and kick above the rolling skin of the water. "MmmMMMMMMMMM, mmMMMMMMMMM, *Ouch! OWWWW.*"

She has accidentally rammed the big toe of her left foot into the opening of the water spout, and now it is stuck.

The Purple Pal floats to the surface of the water.

She tugs on her toe. A drop of blood hits the water with a blip.

"Ow! Ow! Ow!" she says.

It's *sharp* in there!

She pushes her toe farther inside, and then tries to gently pull it back out. A warm crimson stream runs down her leg.

"Ow, ow, OWWWWW!"

Hippie Avenger glances frantically around the room for the something that might help her get her toe unstuck from inside the water faucet. Every move she makes splashes water everywhere, and causes her toe to bleed more.

"Ow, ow, ow, ow, OW!"

She grabs her foot in both hands and pulls. Warm blood gushes. The toe is even more stuck now; the lacerated skin is folded over the sharp edge inside the spout.

Tears run hot down Hippie Avenger's cheeks. This is so painful. This is so embarrassing.

There is no other choice.

"Help!" she cries out. "Help!"

*

From the living room, The Statistician hears Hippie Avenger's cries. He rushes to the bathroom door and asks, "Are you okay in there?"

"No," she says, "I'm not okay."

Through the closed door, she explains what has happened. Well, sort of. She leaves out the orgasm part.

Hippie Avenger tosses the Purple Pal behind the toilet, where it is mostly concealed from view. She tucks a white washcloth between her legs, which covers her pubis more thoroughly than Time Bomb's bikini would, and she holds her breasts in her hands.

"The door is locked," she says. "You'll have to break it open."

With a blow from his shoulder, on his first try, The Statistician smashes the solid wood door right off its hinges. He is stunned for a moment, partly from the shock that he has just knocked a down a door with his own body, and partly because right before him lies the naked and wet body of Hippie Avenger.

When the door came crashing down, Hippie Avenger covered her eyes with her hands. Then she slipped inside the tub, thrashed her free leg to recover her balance, and sent the white washcloth flying.

The Statistician has always wondered what Hippie Avenger's body looks like beneath those Flower Child smocks. Now he knows.

His mouth drops open. Blood dribbles from where a flying hinge bolt smacked his bottom lip.

Hippie Avenger grabs her breasts, then lets one go so she can place one hand between her legs. Three assets to protect, and only two hands to cover them with.

"Can you, um, toss a towel over me or something?" Hippie Avenger says.

"Ah, yeah, sure," The Statistician says, handing her a beach towel, pretending to be fascinated by the faded photo on the wall beside the towel rack.

When her body is more or less covered, The Statistician kneels next to the bathtub and examines Hippie Avenger's trapped toe.

"Ouch," he says.

"Yeah, that's what I said," she says. "Do you think you can get me out of here?"

"I'll try."

He turns on the hot water tap.

"Metal expands when it's heated," he says. "And, thankfully, these fittings are made of iron, which has a much higher expansion rate per degree than, say, brass. Is this too hot for you?"

"I can take a bit hotter, if it will get me unstuck faster."

The Statistician watches the steaming water spiral around Hippie Avenger's leg, clinging to her glistening skin. Her blood has turned the bathwater pink.

"That ought to do," he says, twisting the valves closed with his right hand, and realizing that he's still holding the paper bag from the drugstore in his left. He reaches inside and removes the tube of antibiotic cream, squirts some up inside the water spout.

"This will provide some lubrication," he says, "and maybe help slow the bleeding, too."

With the palm of one hand nestled into the arch of Hippie Avenger's trapped foot, The Statistician takes a firm hold. With the other hand, he grips her captive leg around the ankle. For a guy who uses his brain all day, his hands are surprisingly strong.

"This may hurt a bit," he says. "Are you ready?"

*

SuperBarbie is sure that she just heard a voice.

"You are ready, Gilda Jane," it said. *"You are ready."*

She will cry no longer. She has been unwavering in her faith, and finally God is going to reward her.

"Soon," the voice reassures her.

Gilda Jane lifts the window and tosses out the contents of the paper cup, which she crumples and places in the wastebasket, along with the negative pregnancy-test wand.

She sits down on the bed, with her feet flat on the floor and her back straight, like she's sitting in a pew in church.

She closes her eyes and waits for the miracle.

*

"I'm ready," Hippie Avenger says. By the time she says "I'm ready" again, her toe is free.

The Statistician sits back on the tile floor. "Whew," he says.

Hippie Avenger sits up in the tub, pulls the waterlogged beach towel against her body, and says, "Thanks, mister."

"Any time," says The Statistician, who rises to his feet. His lip is bleeding. His hair is wet. His clothes are soaked from his shoulders to his socks.

Hippie Avenger stands up and steps out of the bathtub, limping on her lacerated foot.

"Do you need some help to walk?" The Statistician asks.

"Well, actually," she says.

He steps toward her. She pulls herself against him.

"I'm getting my blood on you," she says.

"I don't mind. I'm getting my blood on you, too."

"I don't mind, either."

She looks up at him.

He looks down at her.

The wet towel hits the floor with a slap.

Fragrant steam licks from her skin.

She stands on her uninjured foot, wraps the other leg around him.

Their eyes close, but his lips manage to find her lips, her tongue finds his tongue.

He tastes her minty toothpaste.

She tastes his irony blood.

He feels her warm, damp curves.

She feels his …

Wow, Hippie Avenger thinks. *This makes the Purple Pal seem kind of insignificant.*

He pulls away.

"No. I can't do this to her again. I'm sorry. I can't."

He rushes out of the bathroom.

"I'm sorry," he says.

24

KRYPTONITE

"And Kryptonite will destroy him."

— Lex Luthor, on Superman's only vulnerability,
from the movie *Superman*, 1978

Hippie Avenger drapes the wet beach towel over the doorframe in the bathroom.

She kneels on the bath mat, reaches down with her middle finger, and twirls herself the rest of the way to the crescendo, trembling violently, tears running down her face and dripping onto her goosebump-speckled flesh.

"Oh, Gary," she cries, not caring now if anyone hears her, "Oh, Gary, Oh, Gary, ohhhhhhhhhhhhhh."

*

In the bedroom upstairs, The Statistician unzips his pants, unleashes his erection, and strokes it furiously.

"Oh, Karla. Oh, Karla oh Karla oh Karla. Oh God, oh God, oh God!"

The Kleenex box is empty. He grips his penis just beneath the head right before it spurts, and frantically glances around the room. His eyes land on the empty Wicked Weasel bag atop the bedspread, and he pries open the plastic zipper just in time.

"Ohhhh, Karla," he moans. "Oh, God."

*

When she hears a voice crying out for God, Gilda Jane opens her eyes.

Through the slightest crack in the door, she sees Gary in the bedroom across the hall, ejaculating into the plastic bag.

Tears pool in her eyes; they are the opposite kind of tears to the ones she was crying earlier.

Once she's sure that Gary is gone, Gilda Jane tiptoes across the hall and delicately plucks the bag from the garbage can. She lies back on the bed that Gary and his wife have been sharing, and opens herself wide to receive this gift.

When she is finished, she sighs, "Thank you, Lord."

She will never despair again. To despair is to doubt God.

*

Outside, Gary is searching for his wife.

He is going to tell her the truth. He is going to ask her to forgive him. He is going to ask her if maybe they can start again.

She is not sunning on the beach.

She is not swimming in the lake.

The rubber raft sits empty on the line where the grass ends and the stony beach begins. His wife is nowhere to be seen.

But then Gary thinks he hears her voice, making noises he hasn't heard in a long time. He follows the sounds to the cottage driveway, to Miss Demeanor's Subaru Outback.

In the rear window, Gary can see the inflamed tattoo of Wilma Flintstone, swaying back and forth like she's doing a hula dance.

At first he thinks it's a guy with a spiked blue punk haircut who is pleasuring his wife like this, but after he hears a second voice cry out, he knows that it is Miss Demeanor.

Miss Demeanor's tongue and fingers are moving inside his wife. And his wife is pleasuring Miss Demeanor in a similar fashion.

He doesn't want to watch this, but he can't look away. She lifts her head to gasp, and her face appears in the window. He has never seen her wearing this sort of expression before.

Then she sees him.

"Gary!" she shrieks. "Oh my God! Gary! Gary!"

He is already walking away. By the time he has finished walking, he will not know where he is.

His wife wants to kick open the car door and run after him, but Miss Demeanor stops her, holds her in her strong embrace.

"Jessica," she says, "you know it has to end this way."

"I know, Ramona," Jessica cries. "I know."

25

FAST
FORWARD

"To infinity … and beyond!"

— BUZZ LIGHTYEAR, FROM THE MOVIE *TOY STORY*, 1995

What happens next will go something like this:

Shortly after this moment, the kid named Stevie, who works at the local drugstore and who lost his right arm in Afghanistan, will see a man staggering along the road, who he will recognize as OC Douchebag's buddy.

Stevie will drive Gary back to the cottage, just in time for Gary to witness Ramona driving Jessica away in her baby-blue Subaru Outback.

For The Statistician, everything will add up now.

The missing factor will be revealed.

The equation will finally balance.

It will all make sense.

But it won't make sense. Not really. Gary's calculations were way off. He didn't see this coming. Not at all.

Ramona and Jessica will enjoy an intense physical relationship for a while, but Jessica is the monogamous, mate-for-life type, and, well, Ramona isn't. When their affair inevitably ends, Jessica will not be heartbroken. The woman with whom she is really in love is her Spa Buddy, Tricia. Jessica has been in love with Tricia since their first summer together at equestrian camp.

Three months from now, after a day of manicures, hot-stone massages, and a dinner of oysters, truffles, and much champagne, Jessica will kiss Tricia on the mouth instead of on the cheek. And it will turn out that Tricia is in love with Jessica as well.

Jessica's arch-conservative, tobacco-company CEO father will be outraged when his only daughter announces that her girlfriend is moving in with her, but he will not able to do anything about it. To prevent Gary from taking advantage of Jessica's inheritance, he signed the house and trust fund over to his daughter well before her wedding day.

The first real love affair of Jessica's life will miraculously cause most of her respiratory and dermatological sensitivities to vanish, and she will rarely suffer from a migraine again. However, the resulting whispers and titters at the Country Club will cause her father's already prodigious Scotch intake to double, and he will die of liver failure.

Jessica will try to be fair with Gary about their divorce settlement. Although he is entitled to less than nothing under the terms of the pre-nuptial agreement, Jessica will nevertheless present him with a cheque for two hundred fifty thousand dollars.

Gary will tear the cheque in half, hand it back to her, and say, "I was never in it for the money, Jessica."

At that moment, Jessica and Gary will become the friends they were always meant to be.

At Jessica and Tricia's wedding, Cassie will catch the bouquet, and Karla will catch the *other* bouquet.

Aaron and Gilda Jane, The Perfect Pair, will decline the invitation to attend the wedding. The bumper sticker will remain affixed to the back of their minivan: GAY MARRIAGE IS NOT MARRIAGE!

None of the other members of The Indifference League will receive a Christmas newsletter from The Perfect Pair again.

*

Shortly after this moment, The Perfect Pair will head toward home in their white Chrysler minivan.

"Aaron," Gilda Jane will say, "I think it's finally happened. I think I'm finally pregnant. I can feel it. I can feel it!"

"That's wonderful, honey," Aaron will tell her. "I hope you're right." But of course he will hope that she *isn't*, and he will be pretty sure that she's *not*; he's been practically ejaculating *air* all weekend.

Nevertheless, about nine months from now, Gilda Jane's prayers will finally be answered. She will give birth to a beautiful, healthy daughter. The baby will weigh six pounds, three ounces. Gilda Jane will give her a name that reflects her own unwavering faith: Mary Ruth.

Mary Ruth will turn out to be just as athletic as her mother was, but Gilda Jane will downplay her daughter's uncanny mathematical abilities. She will always see Mary Ruth as a direct gift from God, rather than the result of an indirect contribution from Gary.

Mary Ruth will develop abilities far beyond her mother's. She will break provincial, national, and eventually even international athletic records. When she is offered a sports scholarship at a prestigious university, she will not turn it down. When the Olympic team calls, she will answer. Gilda Jane will not see her daughter's success as evidence of Evolution, though; only that Creation is perfect to begin with.

Aaron will turn out to be right about something: as soon as Mary Ruth is born, he and Gilda Jane will rarely have sex again. After Mary's third birthday, when their family doctor determines that Aaron is infertile and always has been, he and his wife will never have sex again.

Eventually, the braces will be taken off Aaron's legs, and he will walk more or less normally again. Gilda Jane will never find out how her husband was really injured in Afghanistan. Contrary to the rumors whispered by soldier's wives at church, and the drunken jokes told by loose-lipped cadets at the canteen, she will continue believe that she is married to a War Hero.

When Aaron is finally promoted to sergeant, he will mercilessly drill his cadets on the training field, and at least one of the female cadets will be drilled with equal vigor by the sergeant in a motel room on the other side of the base. Gilda Jane will believe Aaron when he says he's staying late to do paperwork.

Gilda Jane will be a Believer for the rest of her life, and she will be rewarded with the perfect little home and the perfect little family she's always wanted.

And maybe she will be rewarded in Heaven, too.

*

Shortly after this moment, Fraser and Cassie will turn north and just keep riding, until there are glints of copper in the steel-grey rocks, cliff walls painted pink by the setting sun, the rippling, ghostly sheets of colour of the Northern Lights, and a thousand little silver lakes.

"This is like heaven," Fraser will exclaim over the roar of the Norton Commando's engine.

Cassie will introduce Fraser to her father, the biggest in a town full of big men. Her dad will take an instant liking to the clear-eyed, sandpaper-voiced young man. He used to have a bike just like The Drifter's.

"Can I take it out for a spin, son?" Cassie's father will ask.

"Sure," Fraser will say, "but I need to ask you an important question first."

He will, of course, have already asked Cassie the same question.

Cassie's father will also say yes.

Fraser's brother Gary will be his best man, the way he's always planned it. Karla will be Cassie's maid of honour.

Gary and Cassie will dance together at the reception, and neither of them will feel uncomfortable about touching the other. That was the past, and this is the future.

After a while, nobody will remember what may have happened once between The Statistician and his Protégée. It will seem like a surreal dream that one of them might have had once.

Fraser will work at the copper mine and Cassie will tend bar at the Rockslide Pub until they've saved enough money for their first big trip.

They will travel together for the rest of their lives.

*

Shortly after this moment, Gary will leave the cottage with Karla in her Volkswagen Microbus. He will stay at Karla's apartment, because he can't think of anywhere else to go. Karla will sleep in her cluttered single bedroom, and Gary will sleep under an afghan on the couch in her painting-and-sculpture-filled living room.

Neither of them will actually sleep.

Karla will leave her bedroom door open and all night she will yearn for Gary to come into her room, into her bed, into her. Gary will writhe and sweat all night under the itchy blanket, wishing that he was writhing and sweating with Karla instead. She will want to call out to him, but she will not. He will want to go to her, but he will not.

Three months from now, Karla and Gary will have watched the entire run of Star Wars movies together at the repertory theatre up the street from the gallery where Karla works. *The Empire Strikes Back* will be their favourite of the six films. They will both despise Jar Jar Binks.

One week later, they will watch *Casablanca* together. For a while, Gary's favourite thing to say to Karla will be, "Here's lookin' at you, kid," and Karla will repeat Ilsa's reply to Rick, "I wish I didn't love you so much." Karla will believe that Gary is as cool as Humphrey Bogart, and Gary will believe that she is as beautiful as Ingrid Bergman.

Karla will choose a couple of paintings from the gallery to help Gary decorate his new apartment. She will have doubts about the boldly coloured abstract, but he will hang it in his spartan living room, saying that it "brings the whole place alive."

"Apartment 87," Karla will observe. "A meaningful coincidence?"

"A coincidence, for sure," Gary will say.

A year from now, Gary and Jessica will sign the papers finalizing their divorce. That evening, Karla will arrive at Gary's apartment to find that he has painted his living room purple (not violet). That night they will make love many times on the living-room floor, beneath the abstract painting. When Gary asks Karla to turn around for him, she will hesitate at first, because of the small peace sign she had etched onto her left cheek during a purple-hazy moment at a Phish concert.

"I didn't think you liked tattoos," she will say.

"I love yours," he will reply.

And finally, finally, they will both feel completely satisfied for the first time in their lives. Finally.

And somewhere in between, they will discover that what Gary thinks and what Karla feels are really the same things.

*

Shortly after this moment, the life of the one they all call Mr. Nice Guy will hang in the balance. For the last Not-So-Super Friend left at The Hall of Indifference, the future is unclear.

Within the next hour, Bruce Brown's life will either change dramatically, or it will end dramatically. He will be transformed, or he will be dead; one or the other. It hasn't been decided yet.

Shortly after this moment, Bruce will be floating on the surface of the lake in the raft, staring at the moon and waiting for a sign.

THE ELEVENTH HOUR

"Up, up, and away!"

— Superman, from the TV series
The Adventures of Superman, 1952–1958

Bruce is out in the lake in the raft, staring at the moon and waiting for a sign.

"Have they really left me here all alone?" he wonders out loud.

He's talking to himself. There's no reason not to. There is nobody around to hear him. The rest of the Not-So-Super Friends are gone. They have all fled the scene. The only car that remains in the cottage driveway is Bruce's grey Honda Civic.

"I cooked the meals. I washed the dishes. I built the bonfire. I did everything."

His head is pitched back over the raft's soft stern. The floor ripples as if he's lying on a cheap waterbed.

"And they couldn't even say *thanks* before they all took off. They couldn't even say *goodbye*."

Tears trickle from his eyes and into his ears.

"I bought the beer and the wine. I bought new bedding. I fixed the raft. I did everything."

He sits up. The raft folds in the middle. Cold water sloshes inside.

"I fixed the raft."

He digs his fingernails under the patch that he glued on yesterday, rips it away, tosses it overboard, watches it spiral down into the deep, dark water until it disappears.

He lies back in the raft again. Air hisses through the hole in the rubber next to his left ear.

"If any of you care about me," he says, "come save me."

Maybe at my funeral, SuperBarbie will holler "Amen!" over and over and over again.

Maybe Miss Demeanor will give the eulogy, tell funny stories about me, and make everyone cry.

Maybe Hippie Avenger will break down sobbing when she tries to read a poem about me.

"No!" Bruce hollers at the lake, "Only pricks like Psycho Superstar get that kind of treatment! Fuck! FUUUUUUUUUUCK!"

The last *FUUUUUUUUUUUCK* echoes back from the rock face of the island in the distance, sounding hollow, empty.

Psycho Superstar always said "Nice Guys finish last." Well, no kidding, Jake. Cheers to you, buddy.

Water fills the flaccid raft now.

"They didn't even pass around a card for everyone to sign."

Today is Bruce's thirtieth birthday. His friends have forgotten again.

"Psycho Superstar got to grope their bodies. Psycho Superstar got a bottle of rye."

The boat is almost airless now, and the rubber walls wrap around Bruce as he sinks into the water.

The words burble from his lips as the water covers his face: "Mr. Nice Guy gets nothing."

He's looking up through the rippled surface now.

Bubbles rise from his nose, his mouth, speckle the shimmering membrane above him as his body slowly falls.

The LCD face on his Super G Digital Athletic Chronometer blinks 11:11, on and off and on and off.

Eleven eleven. Eleven eleven. Eleven eleven.

It's supposed to be waterproof to fifty metres. I can't even count on my watch.

Above him, the moonlight is an impressionistic smear, blurred and distorted.

Cold numbs his skin.

Eleven eleven. Eleven eleven. Eleven eleven.

His body is tangled in the deflated raft like a plastic-wrapped cadaver in a morgue.

Darker, darker.

Heavy, sinking. Falling, falling.

Cold, so cold.

Eleven eleven. Eleven eleven. Eleven eleven.

Numb. Sleepy now.

Silence. Darkness.

Peace?

But something cuts through. Something slashing across the surface above him.

Diving. Swimming downward, getting closer.

It's The Drifter.

Of all the Not-So-Super Friends, he's the closest thing to a real-life Aquaman. He was on the Tom Thomson High School swim team. He can swim all the way out to the island and back.

The Drifter has come back to save him.

*

Safely back on shore, Bruce's back is pressed into the soft, cool sand. The others gather around him.

"You gave us quite a scare, mister," Hippie Avenger says.

"We thought we'd lost you, buddy," Miss Demeanor says.

"I'm cold," he tells them.

The two women lie down on the beach and make a Birthday Babe Sandwich, with Bruce in the middle. And he didn't even have to ask.

"Happy birthday, buddy," Miss Demeanor says.

"We love you, mister," Hippie Avenger coos.

They wrap their legs around his body. So warm. So lovely. He holds on to one of Hippie Avenger's breasts with one hand, strokes Miss Demeanor's lean, unadorned back with the other. Her long black hair tickles his face.

262 · RICHARD SCARSBROOK

His stagnant heart begins to throb.

"I want in, too!" The Stunner cries.

"Me too!" says SuperBarbie.

"Let me sit on him!" Time Bomb squeals.

Oh yes oh yes oh yes!

"Hey!" SuperKen grunts, grinding his right fist into his left palm. "You know what happens to guys who mess with other guys' girls!"

SuperBarbie gets up and puts her arms around SuperKen. The Stunner leans against The Drifter. Hippie Avenger stands with The Statistician. Time Bomb is with Miss Demeanor, who once again sports her blue mohawk and all the tattoos.

Bruce is alone on the cold sand again. His ears are ringing.

"The logical thing," says The Statistician, "would be to stop pining over women you can't have. The end result will always be zero."

"Look, Bruce," says The Drifter, "just call Sweetie Pie and tell her you love her, okay?"

"Strike first. Strike hard," says SuperKen.

"Tell her you miss her," The Drifter says. "Tell her that you want her back."

"For once in your life," says Psycho Superstar, "stand up and *do* something about it."

"Are you going to lie there on your back forever?" Sweetie Pie says. "Or are you going to come get me?"

"I'm coming, Alice," Bruce burbles. "I'm coming to get you."

*

Bruce struggles to free himself. He twists and punches and wrestles to escape the rubber straitjacket that binds his body.

He kicks and claws and thrashes, chasing the rising bubbles toward the blur of silver moonlight glowing high above him.

Maybe with just a few more kicks, in just a few more seconds, he will break through the surface, eject the water from his lungs, gasp mouthful after mouthful of sweet, clean air. Maybe he will make it.

Or maybe he won't.

But he continues to struggle toward that pinpoint of distorted light, toward that rippling membrane between life and death. Mr. Nice Guy will fight his way through the cold toward the warmth, through the darkness and toward the light.

It will be the most heroic effort of his life.

ACKNOWLEDGEMENTS

A short story version of "World Domination," called "Bankrupt," was chosen by Heather O'Neill (author of *Lullabies for Little Criminals*) as the winner of the 2009 Matrix Lit POP Award, and was published in the Fall 2009 issue of *Matrix* magazine.

"The Statistician" was shortlisted for the 2012 Vanderbilt/Exile Short Fiction Prize (in the "Experienced Writer" category).

"The Statistician" was also awarded a commendation in the Ireland-based 2009 Seán Ó Faoláin Short Story Competition by judge Philip Ó Ceallaigh (author of *The Pleasant Light of Day*).

"The Statistician" was also longlisted for the 2010 Fish Short Story Prize.

And then finally, "The Statistician" was published in the Fall 2012 issue of *The Puritan*.

"The Eleventh Hour" was published in somewhat different form as "Close to Zero" in the Winter 2010 issue of *Lies With Occasional Truth (LWOT)*.

"Psycho Superstar" was published, as a short story, in the Winter 2010 issue of *PRECIPICe* magazine.

"Miss Demanor" was published in the Summer 2012 issue of *The Toronto Quarterly*.

A modified version of "Time Bomb" was published in the inaugural issue of *The Moose and Pussy*, Fall 2008.

THANKS!

For assistance in helping me research what real commendations would be awarded to this book's fictional hero, Private Steven James, my thanks to Major Carl Gauthier of the Canadian Armed Forces; and my special thanks to the many real heroes of the Canadian Armed Forces, who have earned such honours for real sacrifices.

For her tireless work as my literary agent, my thanks to Margaret Hart of the HSW Agency, and for their respective roles in getting this book into print, my thanks to editor extraordinaire Shannon Whibbs, superstar designer Courtney Horner, and the entire team at Dundurn. For generous support during the creation of this book, my sincere thanks to the Toronto Arts Council and the Ontario Arts Council.

And to all my other Super Friends … as always, thanks for being Super Friends!

For their abundant love, support, and encouragement, thanks as always to my wonderful family, especially my parents, Mike and Judy Scarsbrook.

And, of course, this book is for Bluebell.

AND BY THE WAY ...

All of the characters in the book are, in fact, characters, meaning that they are products of the author's
imagination and do not exist in the real world.

You can find out more about the author and the products
of his imagination at *www.richardscarsbrook.com.*

ALSO ...

The "Indifference League Collector Cards" were inspired by
the Marvel Universe Cards, Series 2. They're pretty cool.

AND ...

The National Geographic feature mentioned in Chapters 17
and 18, "What Darwin Didn't Know," is a real article that
appeared in the February 2009 issue of the magazine.

AND ANOTHER THING ...

The answer to The Riddler's riddle, quoted at the beginning
of Chapter 11, is "a hole," although the author of this book
may have been implying something else.